HALLOWEEN BITES

13 SNACK-SIZED STORIES

2023

FROM BLACK MARE BOOKS

Halloween Bites 2023: 13 Snack-Sized Stories

Black Mare Books

First Edition 2023

This is a work of fiction. Names, characters, places, brands, media, and incidents are either the product of the author's imagination or are used fictitiously. The author acknowledges the trademarked status and trademark owners of various products referenced in this work of fiction, which have been used without permission. The publication/use of these trademarks is not authorized, associated with, or sponsored by the trademark owners.

ISBN: 978-1-959008-35-4

Contents

MOONLIGHTING

By A. B. Richards

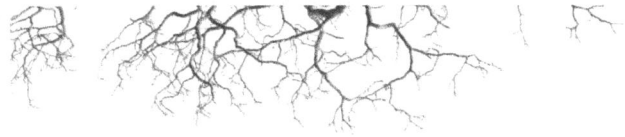

MEAT was a little tough tonight. *Maybe stay out of the low-rent district next time? Nah. That's where the booze is.* I picked a string of gristle out of my teeth and headed back to my office. The moon was one night off full—the rum-runners wouldn't be out this evening, not when the G-men might spot 'em *très facile,* even if the local authorities turned a blind eye.

I strolled along the seawall. I liked the cool Gulf breeze in my hair. The so-called Free State of Galveston apparently ain't heard of autumn.

There was only one case on my desk right now. Missing husband. Wife reported it to the coppers but got the brush off. I felt guilty about takin' her dough. Her old man, Alphonso Kelly, worked at the San Francisco Supper Club. It was an open secret the place was run by the mob, like most of the businesses in this burg. Illegal gambling and liquor brought in so many tourist dollars the local government tended to look the other way.

I stopped and gazed out at the water. White-tipped breakers rolled toward the beach, scratching the belly of the swollen moon that sagged below the horizon. Al Kelly was most likely gator food at this point. Anahuac, across the bay, is teemin' with 'em, and certain gangsters saw the reptiles as a quick and easy way to dispose of their problems.

My bed was callin' my name. I needed to wash up and hit the sack, so I could be fresh for my non-existent clients tomorrow.

I climbed the creaky stairs to the building I call home. A decade before the Civil War, this city was making its reputation as the Wall Street of the South. I was just about to open the door of one of the grand old structures from that heyday. I paused to run my hand over the dark red brick, still vibrant after all this time. Seen better days, no doubt about that. It was one of the few survivors of the Great Storm in 1900. Took a dozen years for the government to basically jack up everything on the island and shove stone and sand underneath it, and I expect this building was one of the last, when everyone was in a hurry to be done with the project. The floors hadn't quite come out level and some of the doors ended up crooked in their frames. But it kept the rent low.

The wooden stairs groaned under my weight. I rented two rooms—the one where I hung my shingle and a tiny apartment on the next floor up.

I paused on the landing. *Qu'est-ce que c'est? Why is the light on in my office?*

Changing course, I found somebody'd jimmied the lock. Standing to the side so I didn't get spotted through the glass, I put my hand on my heater and eased the door open.

A silky female voice called my name. "Laurent?"

"Jubilee? That you?"

"*Oui, oui, monsieur.*" She rose from the shabby armchair and a thick tendril of her long black hair swung over her shoulder. "I need your help."

I snorted. "My help? I find that hard to believe."

She moved closer, metal bracelets clicking in rhythm with sleek hips that swayed under the ruffles of her boxy dress with every step, until her face was inches from mine. "That may be, but it's true."

Her dark eyes drilled into me. I struggled to blink. I tilted my head down to break her gaze. "Did you really just try to mesmerize me?"

She moved back a little. "Sorry, Laurie. Force of habit."

I doffed my fedora. Even in that shapeless floral print, she was a stunner, a real sockdollager. "And how can I help the vampire queen of Galveston on this fine evening?"

Jubilee rolled her eyes. "Wish you'd stop calling me that. I'm only trying to get by, just like anybody else."

"You're not like anybody else. For one thing, you're richer than Jean Lafitte—you stole his treasure that time in New Orleans, *n'est pas?*—and you don't need to shell out for grub." I laughed again. "Your meals pay to come into your lair."

"You make it sound so dark. They don't even remember what happened after they leave the club, just that they had a real fun evening."

"Someday you're gonna get alcohol poisoning from one of those boozehounds."

Jubilee's eyes darkened. "Knock it off, would you? This is serious. They stole my vial."

I swallowed. "The one with dust from your grave?"

She nodded. "If I don't get it back within three days…"

All of Jubilee's 537 years would fall on her head like a ton of avenging angels. "Who is 'they?' Do you know who swiped it?"

"The Grimaldis."

"And you're sure? One-hundred percent? Why would they do that?"

"Why do you think? They want to be my 'business partners' down at the club. I told 'em I didn't need any business partners. Poppy held up my vial, said we both knew exactly how long I had to reconsider. Let me tell you, I don't trust those rotten twins as far as I can spit."

"How many were there? You're way faster and stronger than any of those palookas. Why didn't you just take it?"

"Lu poured holy water on it. I can't touch it. If that wasn't bad enough, they packed it in a crate of garlic with a crucifix nailed to the lid. You see why I need your help."

I chewed the inside of my cheek. "That seems like an awful lot of trouble to go to. No offense, Jubilee, but compared to the Grimaldis, your operation is small potatoes. Why are they so interested?"

"How should I know? It's not like I can afford to call their bluff, is it?"

She had a point. Wasn't like she could go to the cops and report that the local mob kingpins were trying to force her out of her doubly illegal speakeasy and brothel.

Jubilee patted my gloved left hand.

Of course, she'd come to me. I owed her a blood-debt—she'd saved my life years ago, when it was not at all in her best interest to do so. She knew all about the scars I concealed beneath the buttery calfskin, and that casual touch was just her way of calling in the marker.

I gave her a half-hearted smile. "You got a plan?"

"Rats!"

"No plan?"

"Of course, I have a plan. I'm going to use the rats in the building. And a couple other buildings as well. I need a lot of them."

I scoffed. "And what do you want me to do? Deliver a crate of cheese to the Grimaldis?"

"Pack your bags—there's a slot open for you in Vaudeville." Her ruby lips tightened. "Look, I'll get a few rats to move around in the walls so I can listen in and try to learn where they stashed the box. Tomorrow's Mischief Night. Nobody'll think twice about us hanging around downtown."

I raised an eyebrow.

"And if they do, it's Halloween time, ain't it? People running around everywhere pulling pranks, making mischief. Begging for candy is for little kids—that's why they have a different night. Anyway, where was I? Once we figure out where they're holding my vial, I'll send in the rats. Hundreds of 'em. Maybe thousands. The coyotes around here have enough red wolf blood I can control them, too. When the mugs run outside from the rats, the coyotes'll keep 'em occupied. I'll go in with you to show you where the box is. You grab it, and we leg it out of there."

I frowned. "I dunno, Jubilee. There seem to be a lot of moving parts with this plan. I'm not sure that tomorrow night—"

"We don't have much time!" Jubilee snapped. "*I* don't have much time. What do you think? You're just gonna muscle your way in there and take it?"

I sat down in one of the two visitor chairs in my cramped lobby. My feet hurt. "No, not at all. But what if there was a less… attention-drawing way? No way a flood of rats and a growling pack of coyotes won't get noticed, even on Mischief Night." I, for one, certainly did not want the Grimaldis and their goons to bestow an ounce of attention on me. That never ended well.

Jubilee slumped in the other chair. "What's your idea then?"

"Well, I think using the rats to sniff out the location of the box is genius. You can hear what they hear, see what they see, right?"

Jubilee nodded.

"Even if they can't see it, they should be able to smell all that garlic." *Unless…* "Do you think that box Poppy showed you would fit in a safe?"

The vampire licked her lips and shook her head. "No. Not unless it was inside a bank."

"Listen, you get the rodents rolling. See if they can locate that box tonight. Or this morning. It's already tomorrow, isn't it? You get the information, and I'll scope things out during daylight. Then when Mischief Night's in full swing and the Grimaldis have gone to bed, we take back your vial." I yawned. "I'm beat. Gonna have to hit the hay."

"I knew I could count on you, Laurie." Jubilee got to her feet and kissed the top of my head on her way out.

Merde. What have I gotten myself into?

I had enough dough for a cup of joe at the downtown diner, so I headed down the creaky stairs. My sole client, Betty Jean Kelly, nearly bowled me over as I opened the outer door.

"Did you see this?" She shook the morning edition at me.

"Not yet." I squinted. The ends of the glossy platinum-blonde bob peeking out of her white cloche hat practically glowed in the morning sun.

"We've got to go to the police! It might be... Alphonso."

I took the newspaper from her trembling hands. The front page carried an indistinct photo of a pile of ragged, dark-stained clothes lying on the beach. The headline proclaimed, "Mystery Man Murdered!" I skimmed the article. A pre-dawn surf fisherman had stumbled over a corpse on his way down to the water. The law thought the victim couldn't have been in the drink for more than a few hours. He was kinda chewed up, like he'd been used for shark bait. The remains on the beach had been swarmed by crabs, and there wasn't enough left of his face to identify.

"Alright, Betty Jean, you wait down here in the lobby, and I'll run up to my office to get that photo you gave me. Did he have any scars or tattoos, other than the anchor one from the navy?"

She sniffled. "No."

I jogged up the stairs and grabbed the picture. When I came back down, Betty Jean was sitting in a velvet chair, dabbing her eyes. She needed more comfort than I could give her. "Is there anyone you can bring for support? Your mama? A sister?"

Betty Jean shook her head, the tears flowing more freely. "Mama and Papa live in Chattanooga. Sister's in Detroit, brother's in Atlanta."

"I'll go with you. Don't you worry about a single thing."

We took the trolley to the copper's clubhouse. The old City Hall building had looked like some European fantasy when it was new, with turrets, a clock tower, and marble columns. They used to have postcards of the building, it was so fancy. The Great Storm had slapped most of the third floor to the ground. The remaining two stories were patched up good enough for police and fire departments. Guess the city spent all its cash on constructing the seawall and elevating the remains of the town.

Betty Jean and I stepped through the archway and pushed open the heavy door. The building hadn't fallen down in the twenty-two years since the Storm, but it still made me nervous to set foot in the place. Looked like it was held together with spit and baling wire, and whoever'd fixed it up was awful thirsty.

The uniform at the front desk gave me the stink eye. "Awww. It's the baby-faced gumshoe." His words dripped with disdain. "We don't have time to babysit today. Hit the bricks."

"Now that's a laugh. I got a client who's missing a husband. You've got a surplus body."

The copper's eyes narrowed, and I could practically hear the rusty cogs turning. He huffed out a breath and turned to a young man behind him. "Go get Detective Harlan."

Betty Jean and I sat on a hard wooden bench until Mercury Harlan showed ten minutes later. With his slicked-back dark hair, three-piece suit, and blue tie over a crisp white shirt, he looked every bit like Rudolph Valentino from the movies. Even though I'd worked with him many times, I still almost expected an Italian accent any time he opened his mouth.

I introduced him to Betty Jean. He took us to a small room with a table and a few chairs.

"You ain't planning on interrogatin' us, are you Merc?"

He gave us both a quick smile. "Course not! Just thought we could use some privacy, since we're dealing with a... sensitive issue."

Harlan closed the door and sat down. I handed over Betty Jean and Alphonso's wedding picture. "He's also got an anchor tattoo on his upper left arm."

The detective studied the photo. He looked at Betty Jean, then back at the image. "How tall are you, ma'am?"

"Five-two."

"And your husband looks quite a bit taller."

"He was just a pinch over six foot two." A ghost of a smile haunted her lips at the description of his form.

Harlan handed the photo to Betty Jean. "Well, ma'am, you can take comfort in knowing that poor fella from the beach isn't your husband. He wasn't any taller than five foot ten."

"And you checked for tattoos?" I asked.

"That's a bit problematic, given how much of him was missing. I figure he got a snootful and fell into the harbor down at the docks. Plenty of tiger sharks around there in the deeper water. Bull sharks, too."

Betty Jean's eyes widened.

"Sorry ma'am." He got to his feet.

L:

I got some good news, and I got some bad news. The good news is they found it. The bad news is the box is at the Grimaldi's club. Yes, the San Francisco. Don't blow a gasket because it's one of the busiest gin joints on the island and there's people there all hours of the day and night.

It just so happens that Lu and Poppy are going up to Houston this morning. Won't be back 'til late afternoon at the soonest. Heard them talking about it early this morning.

The vial seems to be in a closet, or perhaps a cabinet—some small storage area with a door—in Poppy Grimaldi's office.

I know we talked about tonight, but with them out of the picture for the day, it seems to be a golden opportunity.

Yours,

J

It was almost lunchtime when a young man came into my office and handed me an envelope. I knew the kid—he worked for Jubilee. Once the door clicked shut behind him, I tore open the letter.

I sighed and grabbed my hat. At least the trolley was runnin' this time of day.

The bouncer hung near the entrance like a side of beef. He narrowed his eyes as I approached the door. "Ain't seen you around before."

"I ain't been here before."

He scrutinized me for an uncomfortably long time. I glanced up at the thick cloud cover that cast a watery pall over the intransigent sun and smiled at him.

He held out a meaty palm.

I slipped him a fin, and the bill disappeared into his pocket faster than a fish down a pelican's gullet. He moved out of the way to let me in.

As the heavy wooden door closed behind me, a second-rate jazz quartet started their set. The A-listers, and I mean folks you'd hear on the radio, would play on Friday and Saturday nights. At the San Francisco Supper Club, even the day crowd was fancy. Flappers in their beaded glad rags and their zoot-suited companions left their tables and hit the floor. I edged past the flailing arms and flying fringe to the stairs. Gambling was on the second floor, Grimaldi's offices on the third.

Just to blend in with the crowd, I lost a couple of rounds of roulette before I sneaked off to the stairs. Nobody was around. I had expected there to be some muscle on the lookout, and the abandoned staircase made me uneasy. Something wasn't right. I could feel it in my bones. My senses kicked into overdrive as I crept up to the third floor.

Grimaldi's office was the second door I tried. I listened carefully before I turned the knob. *Was it a bad sign that it was unlocked?* Thick curtains blotted out most of the muted daylight, but a little seeped in around the edges of the fabric. A brass banker's lamp with a green glass shade was the only real light in the room. I stood still, my ears straining to pick up sounds of breathing. I inhaled, trying to catch a whiff of cologne, or perhaps cigars. Nothing that wasn't already driftin' up the stairs from the gaming tables.

I didn't like it, but coming during the day was the best option. In the corner behind the mahogany desk was a door. *A closet? One way to find out.*

Pulling the door closed behind me, I moved across the room slowly, checking for trip wires or other booby traps as I made my way across the expensive rug. The hinges squealed when I pulled the knob. But not as much as I did.

Tied to a chair was none other than Alphonso Kelly. Looked a bit roughed up.

"What the—"

A heavy metal clang echoed behind me, rattling the door in its frame. My heart pounded against my ribs as I crept to the door and put my ear against it.

The floor creaked as people came down the hallway.

I moved to the side as the knob turned and the door was pushed open. No one stepped inside because there was an iron grating blocking the office doorway. I grabbed the bars, trying to shake the cage door open, but it was solid.

Did Jubilee set me up?

Poppy and Lu Grimaldi grinned at me from the other side of the metal gate, flanked by a shaved gorilla the size of Toledo.

Lu pursed her matte-red lips, almost as if she were going to blow me a kiss. "What do we have here?"

Poppy gave his sister a quick side eye before tucking his thumbs into his suspenders. "What are you?"

I scowled. *What kind of question was that?* "I'm a private eye."

He squeezed his eyelids together in a motion that was somewhere between a tic and a wink. "If you say so. Looking for this?"

He tossed a diamond-shaped glass vial into the air and caught it.

"You don't have to answer," Lu purred. "We know Jubilee sent you."

Poppy held up the container and twirled it slowly in front of his face. "You see, we have a problem. I think *you* can be our fixer."

"Me? Why's that? What problem?" I looked over my shoulder toward the guy in the closet. "Is it anything to do with Alphonso Kelly?"

The two gangsters looked at each other. Poppy's eyes cut to me. "Not exactly. We thought he was our mole. But that was not the case."

I scratched my head. "Mole?"

Lu's brow furrowed. "Why are you asking about Alphonso?"

"His wife hired me to find him."

She fixed her eyes on the bound man across the room. "Figures."

Alphonso looked up and grunted as he leaned against his bonds.

"He's a little sore about the misunderstanding." Lu shrugged.

"You better get used to looking after a man." Poppy cocked his head, and I couldn't tell if he was serious or teasing.

That's when I noticed the iceberg on her left ring finger. "When's the happy event?"

She sighed and smiled. "Next Saturday."

Poppy cleared his throat. "Forgive me if I don't open the door so we can sit down and parlay. There's a rat in my organization. He's a shifter. Can look like anybody. So much his own mother couldn't tell the difference. Must be a G-man to boot—some of our shipments have been intercepted. I need someone with a very special set of skills to put the finger on him."

I felt one corner of my mouth tug up into a crooked smile. "How do you know that I'm not the shifter?"

Lu elbowed Poppy. "See? I told ya he'd be smart."

Her brother cringed away from her and nodded as he pressed his lips together, as if choosing his words carefully. "Thing is… we are aware Jubilee has power over vermin. We expected her to eavesdrop on us. She was the only one who could have heard the little fib I told about leaving the Island this morning." Poppy chuckled. "I sell more booze in a day on the lunch shift than Jubilee sells all month. I don't need to horn in on her operation—it'd be more trouble than it's worth. Might have asked her to help us, 'cept she's got one major limitation—a severe allergy to sunlight."

Lu jumped in. "So, I said, 'Who would the toughest gal on the Island call if she was in big trouble?' and it went from there. That wasn't real holy water, by the way. I just nabbed some seawater on the way to her place, so I could splash it on the vial and make it look good."

Poppy spread his arms and grinned. "So, what do you say? You in? I guarantee it'll be worth your while."

"You… you're offering me a job? Wouldn't it have been easier to just come to my office?"

"If we had known who you were." Lu smoothed her skirt. "I figured she would have called in some high-powered genie or something, not a private dick."

I shrugged. "How much does this gig pay?"

Jubilee clutched the vial of graveyard dust to her chest and paced back and forth across my tiny office, her nostrils flaring. "The nerve of those two hoodlums! I ought to—"

"Now, now, Jubilee. I get why you're steamed. Yeah, it was pretty sketchy what they did, but you don't wanna start a war with them. It'll get real ugly for everybody on the Island, but especially us. Besides, they know a lot about you, maybe even where you sleep during the day."

Her eyes narrowed. "Dead men tell no tales. Dead women, either."

"They're payin' *beaucoup* bucks for me to catch this shifter. I was thinkin' that when it's done, I could take an extended vacation. Perhaps go home for a visit—I miss the mountains. You could come with me."

"France is very far away, and you've been gone a long time. Is there anything for you there, other than bad memories?"

Jubilee was probably right. I was just seventeen when she'd found me shivering under a bush, my mother dead a few yards away. The cold night and snow had probably saved my life by slowing the bleeding. Guess the smell of blood had attracted her, so I don't know why she saved me. She never wanted to talk about it. For whatever reason, she bound up my mangled wrist and hand, then took me to her cottage. We were lucky to have the full moon to light our way—the stoney mountain paths were treacherous enough in the day.

Our relationship—well, it was hard to describe. Sort of like family, in that she was my surrogate mother. Sort of like master and apprentice. She taught me about vampires and other curséd things. Once I was back on my feet, we left the mountains. It had grown too dangerous there, and not even Jubilee felt safe, strong as she was. Fear was as much a *bête noire* as any actual beast.

A rumble of thunder derailed my train of thought. "True, it has been a long time. Nonetheless, Gevaudan was my home, and every Creole voice in the streets is like the ghost of some long-lost kin from the Margeride Mountains."

My vampire friend paused her pacing and squeezed my arm. "I know what it's like to miss home so much it hurts. But places have a way of moving on without you. The home you go back to isn't the same one you left, and that makes it even worse."

I gave her a slight smile. "Enough nostalgia. How do we catch this government-issue shifter? The Grimaldis don't have a clue what he is. Makes it hard to figure out where to begin." I tapped a tome in the middle of my desk. "Stopped by the library and got this."

Jubilee picked up the copy of *Grimm's Fairy Tales* and scanned the table of contents. "Not sure this'll help. Doubt the shifter is an evil stepmother or some ragged old man out in the forest."

"You know of any talking fish that could give us a clue, and maybe a golden ring?" I was only half kidding.

Jubilee cocked her head away from me. "Actually... she's not exactly a fish, but she might be able to tell us something. I mean, the shifter's probably fae, and she'd be an expert on that."

The downpour had kept most of the mischief-makers inside this evening, but it meant the sea was extra choppy, splashing our feet as we picked our way along the slick granite blocks of the South Jetty. Salty sea breeze and algae gave the stones a unique fragrance—*eau de poisson*. Fish water. Occasional white splotches, courtesy of the seagulls, intensified the aroma, as well as the slipperiness.

Flickering lightning caromed around the retreating thunderheads, although the sky was still shrouded in thinning clouds. We scrambled along, more than a mile offshore, or at least that's how it felt to me, and I hoped we didn't have to struggle along these slick rocks for the entire six-mile length of the jetty.

Something splashed in the sea to my left, like a dolphin breaching.

"Zara?" Jubilee called.

If I stared hard enough at the frothing water, it seemed faces peered at us out of each rolling wave. Gave me the creeps.

Jubilee shouted again. "Zara!"

The wind laid and the water around us calmed. A human-sized thing surged out of the sea and hove itself onto the jetty.

It was hard to describe. I couldn't say the mermaid glowed, but I could see her clearly in the cloud-sopped dark, almost like some lost ray of sun fell only on her glistening body. Her hair, the golden brown of spring sargasso seaweed, brushed the granite blocks where she sat and surveyed us with silver eyes.

"What brings you two-leggeds out to crawl along the rocks on such a stormy night?" She had the same wicked teeth as a sand shark.

"Looking for you, Zara." Jubilee grinned, her own fangs paltry in comparison.

"You have succeeded in your quest. Is that all?" Zara leaned away from us, as if to slip back into the sea.

"Wait." I took a step forward. "We need information."

"What will you give me for it?"

I had no idea what a mermaid would want, so I turned to Jubilee.

The vampire pulled two gold bangles, inlaid with small topaz stones, from her wrist and handed them over.

Zara smiled as she slid them onto her own arm. "Very well. What is it you wish to know?"

I wet my lips. "We're looking for a shapeshifter. Can mimic specific people. May be a government spy—it's been working in the Grimaldi organization."

Zara chuckled. "Shapeshifter doesn't narrow it down much around here. You might be looking for a kelpie or a nix, if they're of the water clade. Puca and djinn belong to air and fire, and both are excellent shifters."

Jubilee forced a smile. "Thank you for that, but how will we recognize them? And where should we look?"

"They travel the same ships as humans. Seek them at the docks. A kelpie can be sussed out by water-weeds in its hair. The puca's eyes are golden. Nix and djinn are harder to spot, though sometimes the hem of the nix's clothing will be wet."

"Can *you* tell what they are by looking?" I didn't know if Zara would help us any further, but I had an idea, if she was willing.

"Of course!"

"Will you go with us to find him?"

"No." Zara shook her long hair. "But if you go to *The Bleached Barnacle*, that's where you're most likely to meet such folk."

With that, the mermaid dove into the sea, splashing us with her tail.

"Arrgh!" I rasped. "Fancy a pint o'grog?"

Jubilee shook her head. "Is that supposed to be… pirate?"

I studied the slimy granite.

We clambered back to the beach and set off in our wet shoes to the docks.

The *Barnacle*, perched at the end of a fishing pier, hosted a rough crowd. It wasn't easy to tell just by looking which ones were human, and which were something else. Ordinarily, I figured Jubilee and I could take care of ourselves, but I wasn't so sure anymore.

We sat at a wobbly table in the back of the dive, glasses that looked like they'd never been washed sitting in front of us with their sickly amber contents. Even if I drank, I would be afraid to touch that stuff.

"Well, Jubilee? Now what do we do?"

A few eyes wandered over her implied curves, but most focused on the greasy plates or smudged tumblers in front of them.

She closed her eyes. "I'm listening."

I shut my trap. She could detect the heartbeat of a field-mouse a dozen yards away. I don't know how long we sat there. Long enough for my backside to go numb. "Lookit, Jubilee. I think we're gonna have to try again tomorrow."

I started to get up, and her hand shot out to grab my arm. "Stop!"

Her eyebrows knitted together, and her lips squished into a frown. "Come on."

I followed her to a window. Even I could plainly hear Poppy Grimaldi's voice drifting through the screen. "... is the last time. You get your money when it's done, then vamoose. Make like my sister—can you believe the nerve of her? Bringing Joey Conelli into our operation. That greasy weasel'll probably try to poison me at the wedding!" Poppy exhaled loudly. "Nevermind about that. Go sit down with the bloodsucker and that dewdropper she's hangin' out with. Tell them you got the shifter trapped in a shed and you need their help. When you get to the club, bump both of 'em off. But make sure somebody sees you with them here. Ask the barkeep for the time when you order your giggle-water, huh? Get yourself noticed."

Jubilee hissed.

I swore. "This whole thing has been a setup. Seems like he wants to put Lu on ice. He doesn't trust her husband-to-be. Thought there was supposed to be honor among thieves. Or at least among family, anyways."

"Let's go out and speak with 'Lu,' shall we?" Jubilee was already almost to the door.

A woman sashayed toward us, chunky heels clacking on the rough wood of the pier.

I waved. "Hey, Lu."

Her lips curled into a dry smile. "I've been looking for you."

Jubilee crossed her arms. "This doesn't seem like your kind of joint."

Faux Lu shrugged. "Business. I've got some news! Come with me, and I'll show you. I figured it out and trapped him!"

The shifter was good. I really did feel like I was jawing with Lu Grimaldi.

I scanned the pier and street. Not a soul was about. Jubilee put her arm around Faux Lu.

"Hey! Watch it, huh?"

The vamp only smiled. Her eyes glowed red, softly lighting the blank face of her intended prey. Jubilee glanced around, then sank her teeth into the shifter's neck.

It squirmed and changed shape, gasping and groaning. Lu. Something like a deformed merman. A fish. A man. A thick, black eel. Then it turned to water and splashed through the boards of the pier.

"You think it's dead?" I peered through the slits to the rocks below.

Jubilee shrugged. "No idea. If not, it'll think twice about tangling with me again, though." She wiped her mouth. "One down, one to go."

I spotted Poppy crouched by a sky-blue Hupmobile parked across the street. Guess he didn't think I could see him. *Wonder if Lu will pay me for saving her life, since her brother was reneging on our agreement?* I licked my lips. *Looks like the beach crabs'll get another feast tonight.*

The last straggling storm clouds scudded away southward. Light from the full moon fell on my skin like silver fire. I dropped to my knees as bones cracked and re-shaped themselves. My clothes tore and fell away, replaced by thick canine hair. I got to my feet, and the world had taken on the red cast of my wolf-ish vision.

Poppy screamed and fled. He was fast.

But I was faster.

The Break

By A. B. Richards

We always went camping over the weekend closest to Halloween. This was a far better way than just turning off the porch light to avoid blowing *beaucoup* bucks passing out candy to the greedy little rug rats of random strangers. And late October, when it starts to cool down, but isn't yet cold, is the perfect time for a break from the rat race.

It was usually the same four of us: Jesse and Cindy, Steve, and me. We'd met at college and stayed friends for over a decade. Significant others had come and gone, but so far, none had lasted more than a couple of years. Steve and I were in the wedding party when Jesse and Cindy got married. Cool outdoor venue, with cabins and a lodge, miles of hiking trails. We had the place to ourselves for the rest of the weekend after the lovebirds left on their honeymoon.

Which would have been great, if I hadn't had to run Steve to the ER. He never said a word to anybody, but the day Cindy married Jesse broke his heart. We both got drunk, and he stabbed himself. You wouldn't believe how fast a jolt of adrenaline can sober you up. The honeymooners knew Steve got hurt, but neither of us told them what really happened. It was an accident as far as they knew.

Jesse and Cindy sat in the middle row of the SUV. I'd folded down the back seats for more room to stow our gear. Steve rode in the passenger seat. He was supposed to be the navigator. I noticed him staring into the rearview mirror several times.

"You okay, man?"

"Huh? Yeah. There was a car. Thought it was following us, but it turned off."

"Ah. Hey, Cindy? Could you pass me a soda?"

"Sure, Chris." Icy water dripped off the can she handed me from the cooler that sat on the floor between her and Jesse.

Steve opened it and set it in the drink holder for me.

"Thanks."

The conversation ebbed and flowed over the two-hour drive to the Big Thicket National Preserve. The 'thick' in 'thicket' should be the first clue. The park is a dense forest, with the Neches River running through it. A few bayous drain into the river, and they're dotted with cypress swamps. Green duckweed covers the water and cypress knees jut above the swamp like broken teeth. I get that they're specialized roots that keep the trees from drowning, but they look spooky, and they can make it hard to navigate in a canoe or kayak. Plus, you never know if one of those bumps in the water is actually going to turn out to be an alligator. I stay out of the swamp.

We were headed to the Canyonlands Unit for some back-country camping. Very primitive area, and we rarely saw any other campers when that was our destination. Downside is sometimes hunters stray into the park. That only happened once, and they were okay. I think they really knew they were in the park, though. Some units in the preserve do allow hunting. But not Canyonlands.

Night hiking is a bad plan—there are bluffs along the river. If we survived the fall, walking off a cliff in the dark would land us down in the river flood plain or a cypress slough. Where the gators live.

There are a crazy number of wild animals in these woods. Guess they know about the hunting ban. Once a raccoon fell out of a tree on Jesse and Cindy's tent during the night and scared the crap out of everybody. And a 'possum got into the crackers

Steve brought one year. His fault for leaving them outside the tent. We've spotted deer—well, antlers moving through the trees. Funny thing is, they sound like someone shouting "Yeah!" when they do make a noise. That's... disconcerting. Not as much as a screaming bobcat, but animals are noisy, what can I say?

Jesse and I dragged a huge limb into camp. Park rules forbid chopping down trees or limbs, but any dry, dead limbs that have fallen on the ground are fair game. Steve picked up a hatchet to cut it into campfire-sized pieces.

"I went to an ax-throwing party. Birthday for somebody at work. You guys tried it?"

I shook my head. "I've seen places for it, but never done it."

Jesse chuckled. "Did it once at RenFest. Cindy kicked my ass at the archery booth, but neither one of us were great at tossing an ax."

I wiped my hands on my jeans. "RenFest? Does that make you a Renaissance man?"

"Hold off on the dad jokes until you have kids, okay?" Jesse rolled his eyes.

While Steve chopped wood, the rest of us got everything ready to cook. We usually feasted on Friday night, hiked and explored Saturday, and stopped for a big breakfast on our way back into town on Sunday. Anything perishable had to be cooked as soon as we got the fire going when we arrived, so we made the most of it.

I'd already prepared my foil-pack garlic fries before we hit the road. It was my signature dish, although I did bring supplies to make s'mores tonight and baked beans tomorrow.

It got dark fast in these thick woods. Steve hurried to stack the wood and start the fire. He paused and looked around. "Did you hear that? I kinda feel like we're being watched, and I thought I heard something moving in the brush."

I scanned the campsite. "I didn't hear anything."

"Where did the noise come from?" Cindy switched on her mega flashlight.

Steve pointed to his left. "Over there."

We all turned our heads in that direction. Nothing.

Steve frowned.

Cindy moved the beam of the flashlight up into the branches of the clump of trees. Glowing eyes peered down at us. I dropped my koozie.

Jesse laughed. "There's your dark watcher. It's just a gray fox."

"In the tree?" Steve snorted.

"Sure." Cindy lowered the flashlight. "They sleep in trees to avoid predators. Even make dens up there. He's probably getting ready to go find his own dinner."

"Alright, Jeff Corwin." Steve resumed stacking the wood.

I was tired from the long drive and stuffed with food.

"You asleep, Chris?" Jesse asked, louder than he really needed to.

"No. Just resting my eyes." That's what my dad always said when he was drowsing off and didn't want to admit it. Oh, well. Wouldn't be the first time my friends thought I sounded like an old fogie.

"Just go to bed." Cindy tossed a twig into the dying campfire.

"And miss all the fun?"

Jesse yawned. "We'll put the fire out. You and Steve can crash. You two are on fire duty tomorrow."

I thought Cindy said something along the lines of "caper chart," but I was yawning so much it drowned out her words. I considered just crawling over to my tent, but I figured I'd never hear the end of it. Plus, there were a lot of pinecones lying around. My knees cracked when I got to my feet.

Steve stood facing the trees, a few feet behind our tents.

"Man, that's way too close to the campsite to be taking a leak."

"What? No. Thought I heard something, and I was just checking it out."

"Like what?"

"Voices, maybe. Hard to tell."

"Probably deer. They make weird sounds."

"Maybe."

I crawled into my tent. It was too hot for a sleeping bag just now, but I might want it later. I unzipped it and lay on the bottom half, the top scrunched against the tent wall. I was asleep pretty much the instant I got still.

I'm not sure of the exact noise that dragged me out of sleep. Footsteps shuffled through the leaves around my tent. I reached for my flashlight. It was as good a weapon as it was a light source. Had to be one of the others heading out into the forest for a bathroom break. The footsteps stopped, and I laid my head back down. My eyes snapped open as I heard a new sound.

Slowly, the zipper of the tent flap parted. *What the hell?* My pulse raced and my breath quickened. I put my thumb on the flashlight switch. The second a face appeared, I turned the light on, blinding the intruder with high intensity LEDs.

Steve put his hand up to shield his eyes. "Jeeze, Chris! What's gotten into you?"

"*You* were the one sneaking into *my* tent." I lowered the light.

"Yeah. Because you kept calling me. I thought you might be sick or something."

"I don't know who was calling you, but it wasn't me. I was out cold. Until you woke me up."

He pursed his lips. "Fine. Whatever. I'm going back to bed. See you in the morning," He grumbled. Steve zipped up my tent flap, and moments later, his own.

Thanks a lot, Steve. I was wired now from the adrenaline that surged through my veins when he scared me awake. And now that I was awake, I had to pee.

I got up and took care of my business, then I sat cross-legged on the edge of the tarp I had placed under my tent and looked at the stars. In the city, it was easy to pick out Orion. Polaris. The Big Dipper. Those stars shone the brightest and cut through the light pollution of civilization. But out here, the night sky looked like someone had spilled a bottle of glitter, and I couldn't find my old friends. I sat there watching for shooting stars—this was the peak of the Taurid meteor shower—until my butt started to go numb. I climbed back inside my nylon shelter and finally drifted off to sleep.

"Wake up, lazybones!" Jesse scraped his fingernails along the top of my tent.

I groaned and wiped a string of drool off my jaw, squinting in the bright morning light that filtered into my tent. Not how I'd intended to start the day.

"I'm coming." I yawned and grimaced at the rush of morning breath that suddenly overwhelmed my tiny space.

I crawled out of my nylon nest and stretched my stiff joints. The water was already on the boil for the instant oatmeal that would be our breakfast. Steve and Jesse studied the park map while I brushed my teeth and splashed water on my face.

When I joined the group, Cindy and Jesse were acting weird. They kept looking at each other and making faces.

Jesse cleared his throat. "We wanted you to be the first of our friends to know."

Cindy grinned. "We're expecting a baby in the spring!"

Steve and I hugged and congratulated them. I felt guilty for being bummed that this would most likely be our last camping trip for quite some time. Maybe the last one ever.

After we cleaned up from our meal and extinguished the fire, we grabbed the food we were planning to eat for lunch and hit the trail. The weather was perfect. Low seventies, low humidity. Clear skies. The satisfying crunch of dry leaves under our boots. Much of our hike was in the cool shade of thick forest. There were no maintained trails, just barely-there old logging roads that the woods had taken back with a vengeance over the past ninety years. Jesse navigated us with a compass.

We got back to camp just after 4:30. That gave us two hours before sunset to rest and get dinner going. Steve and I gathered more wood while Cindy and Jesse got the food ready for the fire.

Steve bumped into me. "Did you see that?"

I paused my stick snapping. "See what?"

"Something ducked behind the tree over there."

My eyes followed his pointing finger. Nothing moved around the tree. Still carrying the rotten stick, I walked over there and circled the tree. I looked up. "Nothing here now. Probably just a squirrel."

We finished gathering firewood, although Steve was much more skittish than usual. His nervousness rubbed off on me because I startled at every rustle of the leaves.

At the campsite, Steve pulled out the hatchet and cut the bigger limbs down to size. I helped him carry the wood over to the fire ring we'd made. We'd been overly enthusiastic in our wood fetching because we had a substantial amount left over. I gathered it up and stacked it away from the fire in case we wanted to use it later.

The flames were eating up the kindling, and Steve came over to where I stood by the woodpile.

He raised the hatchet, gesturing to a fallen log. "Watch this."

Steve threw the ax, and it somersaulted across the clearing, blade biting into the tree with a meaty thunk.

While we waited for the food to cook, he gave us hatchet-throwing lessons. Cindy and Jesse took turns minding the food. By the time the potatoes were soft, twilight was closing in and my arm was sore.

Cindy banged a metal plate with a spork. "It's ready. Get your plates."

I thought Steve was right behind me, but when I turned to check, he faced the woods, hands smashed against his ears.

"Leave me alone!" Steve shouted at the inky forest. He looked at Cindy, then Jesse and me, his eyes pleading. "Don't you hear it?"

"What are we listening for, Steve?" Jesse stepped closer to his wife.

"My name. They keep. Calling. My name." His voice cracked as he spoke, and I thought he might burst into tears.

"Steve?" Cindy's voice was soothing. "Perhaps you're just over-tired. Why don't you get some rest?"

He took a step backward, and nearly tripped over the wood pile. "Why do you want me to go to sleep? You're not... working with *them*, are you?"

Steve whipped his head around to face me. His eyes were wild.

And that's when it hit me. The voices. The things hiding in the trees. They were all in his head. *Crap. He's having a psychotic break.*

I swallowed hard and tried to keep my voice calm. "Hey, Steve? What are you doing with that hatchet?"

Steve said nothing. He was pale and sweat beaded on his forehead.

"Steve?"

He cocked his arm back and hurled the ax. I wanted to move, but my muscles didn't seem to get the signal to run from my brain. I just stood there and watched the hatchet tumble end-over-end toward me.

TRICK

By A. B. Richards

THE house had not been there yesterday.

But this morning on the way to drop the kids off at school, there it was, like it had fallen straight out of the artist rendering of our master-planned community, with the requisite two trees staked in the front yard and a mailbox that matched every other one on the street. Pumpkins on the front porch added a pop of color to the greige exterior, accented with blue-grey trim. Bright fall-themed cushions adorned the loveseat and two chairs, which were framed by bamboo plants in large silver pots.

They were still building houses in our section, but overnight?

When I got home, I texted my husband. "Rick, did you see the new house at end of the block this AM?"

It took him a little while to get back to me. "No. It was dark. Did they pour the slab last night?"

"More than that. It's done."

He responded with a surprised emoji. "Did you turn the wrong way out of the drive again?"

I responded with a tongue-sticking-out emoji. "No"

The dog's wagging tail flopped against my leg. Black hair puffed in little clouds every time she made contact. She was a seventy-pound shepherd mix we had gotten from the pound, and I never worried about a thing when I was walking her. "Hey, Pepper! You need to go pee-pee?"

I snapped the leash on her collar and picked up the poop bag dispenser. We set out in the direction of the overnight house. As we approached, my fellow dog walker, Annabelle, stood in front of the new structure, her English bulldog snuffling beside her. As usual, her hair was pulled into a messy ponytail, and, since it was chilly this morning, she wore sweatpants that were perhaps a bit too snug.

A Maserati with dealer tags sat in the driveway of the instant house, and I wondered if the whole thing was just a hologram projected on a 360° screen. Some new kind of advertising, perhaps? Which did seem weird, because houses in this neighborhood were being snapped up faster than they could be built.

"What do you make of this?" Annabelle asked when we came even with her.

I shrugged and leaned over to pat her dog. "Hello, Edgar."

The front door opened, and I straightened up. *So much for the hologram theory.*

A woman in a designer tunic and expensive yoga pants stepped onto the porch. Her blonde, beachy waves fell just below her shoulders. A gem-studded watch glittered on her wrist as she smoothed her thick hair over her shoulder. "Hi! I'm Elizabeth. We just moved in last night."

"It's… um, nice to meet you. I'm Jessica. I didn't even notice any moving trucks yesterday." *Or a house.*

"Yes. Your house went up amazingly fast. I'm Annabelle, by the way."

"Well," Elizabeth smiled at us. "You know how builders are. The faster they build them, the faster they can sell them."

Her voice was flat, devoid of any accent. It sounded almost… synthetic. But that was ridiculous. Even computer-generated voices are based on the voices of real people. "Welcome to the neighborhood, Elizabeth. Where are you from?"

"We're new in town."

Annabelle shifted her weight. "You have kids? Brighton Elementary is top rated. It's across the street from the neighborhood."

"Yes. Devon and Ashe are already enrolled."

Pepper sat down and I leaned over to scratch her ears. "Oh? What grades are they in?"

The way Elizabeth tilted her head and gazed at us before she spoke made me uncomfortable.

"Devon is in second and Ashe is in fourth. Would you like to come inside for coffee?"

Pepper got up and flicked her ears forward, staring at Elizabeth. The woman looked like she was on her way to an ad campaign photoshoot for luxury goods—a poster child for conspicuous consumption—but something about her just creeped me out. "We need to finish walking the dogs. Maybe next time. Well, guess I'll see you at the PTO meeting. Nice meeting you." I waved and started walking briskly down the block.

Edgar trotted after Pepper, dragging Annabelle with him. "Jessica!" she hissed as we paused at the end of the block for a car to pass. "We could have had coffee. She was just trying to be friendly."

"Yeah, like a spider invites a fly into its parlor. There's something off about her. And that house! It was. Not. There. Yesterday. You can't ignore that."

"Well, it could be prefab. You can buy house kits on the internet, you know. I'm going to tell River to make a point of befriending Ashe. It's only neighborly. They're new."

"We're *all* new, Annabelle. The subdivision only opened in May. And even with a kit, you can't put up a house overnight. You still have to get permits and inspections and stuff."

Annabelle stopped to give Edgar a drink of water from her bottle. "Mobile homes have come a long way. Some of them, you can't even tell they're manufactured. And *you* were new two months ago. You didn't seem to be offended when I started talking to you."

We resumed our walk. "I'm glad that you did. I like you. *You* are not creepy."

"Elizabeth is creepy because she's stunning?"

I sighed. "About that. Even if they did allow mobile homes here, does Elizabeth look like someone who'd live in a trailer, even a fancy one? Seriously, I didn't mean to offend you. She gave *me* a weird vibe. You didn't get one. Let's just agree to disagree about Elizabeth and talk about something else."

"Fine. What do you want to talk about?"

Over the next two blocks, we planned a trip to the Mostly Ghostly Halloween store for last-minute costume props. Well, props for her. Costumes for me. Annabelle is very artsy-craftsy and had made River's elaborate steampunk costume from scratch. Me, I couldn't sew a button.

On Friday, the kids were allowed to wear their costumes for a playground parade first thing in the morning, then they had to take them off and go back to a normal school day, so parents had to be there to collect the outfits. And take copious photos.

Saturday would be the big day. Several churches had "fall fun fairs," stores at the local mall were passing out candy to kids in costume, and of course, the *pièce de résistance*, actual trick-or-treating in the neighborhood.

I tried not to grin too broadly as we walked into Mostly Ghostly. Halloween had always been my favorite time of year, and I felt like a kid in a candy store. I shepherded Molly and Blake to the children's costume area, while Annabelle and River headed to the adult section to find goggles and a pocket watch.

Against the rear wall, I spied the motion-activated decorations. Since I could still see the kids from there, I strolled to the back of the store. As I neared, a werewolf with a bloody mouth and tattered pants growled at me, his eyes glowing red. A warty green witch cackled maniacally, beckoning to me with a long, crooked finger from behind her steaming cauldron. A zombie baby snarled as his head turned 180° to glare at me with empty eye sockets.

"Mom!" Blake waved a packaged costume at me.

I hurried back to my offspring and examined his choice. It was a bodysuit that would cover him from head to toe. Bones were printed front and back to give the illusion of a skeleton scampering around without its skin. I eased the package from his clutches and replaced it with a larger size.

"Finding anything you like, Mols?"

She frowned as she shook her head.

Molly's personality was more goth than girly, but even the 'scary' girls' costumes were uncomfortably short, syrupy sweet, or ridiculously cartoonish.

"You know, you can look in the boys' section."

"Guess I'll have to."

Blake trotted off to find River, and I stayed with Molly while she pored over the racks of packaged disguises.

She finally settled on a ninja outfit. "I need a sword, Mom."

"Sure." We headed to the bins of faux swords and axes. I perused plastic skeletons while she sorted and sifted through the edged weapons. She found a barbarian blade, and I nabbed a 6' werewolf skeleton to add to my holiday décor. I gazed longingly at the animatronics behind me, but we had just bought a new house and furniture, and I couldn't really justify spending that much on decorations at this time. But maybe there'd be an end-of-season sale...

The kids had had a blast at the fall fun fair and pumpkin patch down the road from us. They'd gotten to decorate mini pumpkins and there was a photo spot with stacks of normal-sized pumpkins. I had told them they could trick-or-treat at the mall or in the neighborhood, but not both. They complained, but by the time we were rounding the final block to our house, they were tired and starting to get cranky.

Across the street, Elizabeth's porch light was on. The walk to her front door was lined with pumpkin luminaries, and the same animatronic witch I'd seen in Mostly Ghostly, with her bubbling cauldron and curling finger, sat silently on the porch, waiting for an unsuspecting tot to trip the motion activation.

Our group of children returned, and the clump of parents migrated to the next house. I did not want them to ring Elizabeth's doorbell, and the closer we got to the Better-Homes-and-Gardens-ready place, the more my fight-or-flight response tried to take over. If any of the other parents were feeling it, they covered it well.

When the kids rejoined us, I said, "Mols? Blake? If you guys are tired, we're almost home. We can call it done for the night. Look at those bulging trick-or-treat bags you've got."

While Annabelle shot me a hopeful look, Molly made eye contact with her brother.

Blake and River turned and counted lit porch lights together. "There's only seven more houses, Mom. We can do it."

The next house was Elizabeth's. I warned the intrepid ToTers about the witch, and the band of monsterlings clustered together as they took the three steps up to the front door. When the cackling started, they shrieked, then laughed. Elizabeth, dressed in a Morticia Addams-style mermaid dress, opened the door. Even out of the direct shine of the streetlight, I could tell the two dads in the group were gawping at her. She waved at us parents, and I could feel her eyes singling me out. We finished the last six houses and hurried home to evaluate the haul.

There weren't many unexpected finds. A few coins. A small box of raisins. A bouncy ball. The rest was a mountain of candy. Every variety was familiar, even the off-brands.

Every variety but one.

Molly and Blake both had two. The wrappers were orange with black stripes. But there was no writing of any kind. No logos or pictures.

I waved my husband over. "What do you make of these, Rick?"

He turned them over in his palm and raised an eyebrow. "Very mysterious. I'm going to go out on a limb and guess that it's candy."

My parents had grown up with hospitals offering to X-ray candy for razor blades, just in case, after a kid ate poisoned Pixy Stix, and they had instilled the dangers of Halloween candy in me.

The fact that the boy's own father did it for an insurance payout didn't dampen the panic. Not even for me, and I knew the story.

I looked from Molly to Blake. "Do you remember which house they came from?"

Blake shrugged.

"The vampire lady gave them." Molly nodded. "Just down the street."

"Aaah!" The candy flew from Rick's hand. "It moved!"

"What moved?"

"The candy. It popped up in my hand. Like one of those Mexican jumping beans." The kids scrambled away from their horde.

Rick chuckled. "Maybe it's prank candy from a joke shop. I mean, you can get anything on the internet these days. Or, could be a larva of some kind in there. Why don't you seal it in something and we'll see what crawls out?"

Blake nodded enthusiastically.

I picked up the mystery morsels and got a glass food storage bowl from the kitchen. I unwrapped the candy, put all four pieces in the dish, and snapped on the lid.

The treats were nondescript chocolate-esque squares. They began to squirm and hop inside the bowl, moving faster where my hands warmed the glass and slower where the surface was cooler.

"Okay." I set the dish on the table and turned to the kids. "Choose three pieces of candy, then brush teeth and hop in bed."

Rick walks Pepper on the weekends. I work part time from home, so my schedule is flexible, but my time isn't entirely my own. This weekend, I had groceries delivered and did meal prep for the week, so it wasn't until Monday that I saw them.

Silver pots of bamboo, and brightly colored fall-themed outdoor chair cushions had appeared on several front porches. Or on decorative front yard benches of houses without porches, even if benches had not been there before.

I guess Elizabeth's style is trending now. Wonder how many more houses are going to pop up like mushrooms overnight? Pepper paused to irrigate the grass. Edgar, trailed by a strange figure, saw my dog and began to trot toward us.

As they neared, I saw that the person with Edgar was, in fact, Annabelle. She was wearing a black plastic sauna suit. She'd dyed her unruly chestnut hair blonde, and it was slicked into a severe high ponytail, not a flyaway to be seen. And did she have on… lipstick?

"I hope you don't give yourself a heart attack or heat exhaustion in that outfit."

Annabelle wiped her sweaty forehead. "River's in fourth grade now. It's time I finally lost that baby weight. I also started the Beverly Wood Diet. Everyone who's anyone is doing it."

"Oh. Good for you."

We continued our walk, mostly talking about the new fourth-grade teachers, Mr. McCallum and Ms. Johnson. Edgar only needed half as much walking as Pepper, so as we looped back toward Annabelle's house, I did a double-take.

A silver pot, bamboo rising gracefully out of it, sat next to a bench with a colorful fall-themed cushion on her front porch.

Annabelle must have seen me staring. "Looks nice, doesn't it? Very contemporary and chic."

"Yes. It's certainly… modern. See you tomorrow?"

Annabelle's eyes slid to Edgar. "Uh, I.. um. I'm having coffee with Elizabeth tomorrow morning."

"Oh. Well, that's very neighborly of you. Have fun." I started to walk away, and then a crazy thought hit me. "Annabelle? Do you recall whether River had any strange-looking candy? Orange with black stripes, kinda square?" I measured about an inch with my fingers.

She shrugged. "No idea. Sorry. Why? Was there something wrong with it?"

"I'm not sure. See you later."

As soon as I got home, I checked the online appraisal district listings for Elizabeth's address. I frowned. The county reported it as an unimproved lot owned by Bay Tree Builders. *How long does it take for the records to update?*

I remembered the glass container, which had been shoved to the back of the countertop. I picked it up and brought it close to my face. There was definitely something crawling around in there.

I jumped as a small grey blob leaped at my face. It stuck to the glass, its tiny… were those tentacles? Whatever they were, they splayed out like a slimy daisy. I found my reading glasses and tried to get a closer look.

Three more slithered from behind their abandoned candies and also launched themselves at the side of the container.

I nearly dropped the dish. The things looked like tiny octopuses, only with about twice as many tentacles. And no eyes. Basically, snot blobs with arms. I snapped some pictures with my phone and sent one to Rick before uploading them to a couple of Facebook groups I was in, hoping for an identification.

I picked up the kids from school and asked the same question I asked every school afternoon for the past nine years. "How was your day?"

Blake groaned. "Terrible."

"Oh? What happened?"

"I don't know. I mean at recess, River wouldn't even play the superhero game we usually play. He went over to play kickball with George and the rest of those guys. He never hangs out with them." Blake sniffled. "He said games where you have to use your imagination are dumb."

My heart hurt for my kid. "Sorry to hear that. Did you have a fight or anything?"

He shook his head. "No."

"What about you, Mols? Kids seem any different?"

"Not really. Well, Brian was acting weird."

"How so?"

"He talks back to the teacher and has to get sent to the office all the time. But he did everything she said, and even helped Sarah when she tripped and fell on the way to the music room."

"How about that."

The kids were in the living room having a snack when there was a knock at my door. I looked through the peephole. Two men in dark suits stood at my door, a freckled redhead and a blond. A black SUV with dark-tinted windows was parked in front of my house.

"Can.. I help you?" I asked through the door.

"Yes ma'am," the blond said. He held up a printout of the photo I'd put on my bug group to identify the snot blobs. "Jessica Valdez?"

"Who are you?"

They held up official badges from the Department of Agriculture. "Ma'am, you seem to have stumbled across an invasive species. It's very toxic and dangerous. Do you still have the specimens?"

I had no idea the USDA had these kinds of employees. I opened the door. "Sure. Come in." I was eager to know what those nasty little critters were.

I led them to the kitchen and handed the redhead the glass bowl. "What are they?"

"They're an invasive species." The blond gave me a fake smile.

"Yeah. You said that. I just want to know—"

"Is this all of them?" Blondie seemed tense.

"Yes."

"You're sure?" His brows bristled above grey eyes.

"What's that in the jar with them?" The redhead seemed nicer.

"That's the candy they came in.

The agents exchanged a glance, and the redhead nodded. "And where did the candy come from?"

"Halloween. I can show you the exact house."

"Please do."

"Hey, Blake? Mols? I'll just be gone a minute. If you want, you can get the controllers out and play a game until Daddy gets home from work."

They nodded and Blake raced for the TV stand cabinet.

The blond stopped a few feet away from the front door. I used my phone app to lock it as I followed the redhead to the SUV. He still had the glass dish in his hands. The liftgate opened, and he slid my container of snot blobs into a metal box and locked it. Two men in tactical military gear were in the driver and passenger seats. Another two were in the back row. I didn't think these people were really from the USDA anymore.

I pointed to the left. "This way. House is at the end of the block. Number's 3232."

We passed the metal behemoth and stood on the sidewalk.

I wanted to cry with frustration—3232 was a vacant lot. Not a hint that a house had been there yesterday.

"It was here. I swear. The woman's name was Elizabeth. I'm telling you, the house just appeared overnight. My friend said it was a mobile home they hauled in. They'd planted trees, for Pete's sake! I'm not crazy!"

"It's okay, Ms. Valdez. We're very grateful you discovered these invasive exotics and turned them over to us."

In my desperation to convince him I hadn't lost my mind, I told him about Annabelle. The silver pots of bamboo. The bright cushions. The kids acting strangely at school.

He turned back toward the house, and I remained where I was. "What are those things?"

Red pursed his lips and let out a breath, then stepped closer to me, as if he didn't want to be overheard by the neighbors. "They're parasites. They enter the sinus passages through either the nose or mouth and attack the prefrontal cortex. It's similar to a lobotomy, but not exactly. It manifests as more of a hive mind, like wasps. They're controlled by... let's call it the queen. They're all pieces of a biological machine, now. Every trace of individuality is wiped away."

"That's terrible! If you kill the snot blobs, people will go back to normal, right?"

His shoulders drooped. "Snot blobs?" He pointed over his shoulder. "You mean the parasites? I'm afraid not. The damage is permanent."

I thought of poor Annabelle and a tear traced its way down my cheek. Elizabeth had really put the 'trick' in trick-or-treat.

"So, what are you going to do about it?"

"We're going to have to decontaminate the area."

The kids had been tucked into bed. Pepper was curled up next to the couch. Rick and I stared in horror at the news on the TV in the safehouse. Our master-planned community was on fire. The gates had somehow become jammed and no one could get out. A helicopter flew over, futilely dumping fire retardant on the raging flames.

Rick put his arm around me and pulled me close. He looked up at Red. "How long are we going to have to stay here?"

"That depends. The thing that you know as Elizabeth knows who you are. This nest has been destroyed, and she won't stop hunting you. Unless you can help us catch her."

"What is she? What does she want?

Red shook his head slowly. "I'm sorry. That's classified."

I laughed bitterly. *We weren't being rescued. We were bait.*

Queen for a Day

By A. B. Richards

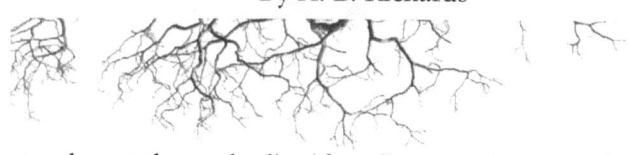

S YRAH almost threw the liquid eyeliner applicator at the mirror. Her third attempt at the thick, smooth line on her top lid was even worse than the other two. She frowned at the glass while she reached for makeup removal pads. She still had a couple of weeks to practice before someone, preferably her, would be crowned Miss Chicory, Queen of the Harvest Festival.

She knew Kayleigh Marrs, her biggest competition for the crown, wouldn't make such a beginner-level mistake. Just last week, Syrah had applied perfect cat eyes without a second thought. Then she spent most of the money she'd scraped together babysitting on the entry fee for the Milbyville fall pageant. Now her best efforts looked like a three-year-old had gotten into their mother's cosmetics.

"Seer?" Mogen's voice was barely above a whisper.

Syrah forced a smile as she turned to her pre-schooler sister. "What do you need, sweetie?"

"Mommy's still sleeping, and we're all hungry."

Good job, Debra. Syrah's jaw clenched as a wave of fury at her mother rolled over her. She got to her feet. "Let's see what's in the pantry."

Her six-year-old brother, Boone, and nine-year-old sister, Chardonnay, got up from the show they were watching and followed them into the kitchen. Debra was passed out on the couch, drool dribbling down her chin as she snorked and snorted in her booze-soaked stupor. Syrah resisted the urge to stomp over there and shake her awake. It was only a matter of time before

Debra woke up screaming, anyway. Syrah could tell by the way she twitched.

Instead, she led the unmerry band into the kitchen. "Margarita back from work yet?"

Boone shook his head.

Her next younger sister worked in the store at the truck stop. She sometimes ended up with a double shift, which was fine during the summer, but not so good once school had started. The sophomore's grades had slipped from As and Bs to solid Cs, and they were only two months in. Syrah would have a talk with her later.

She sighed and opened the pantry.

A can of chickpeas.

Half a bag of tortilla chips.

A can of mushroom soup.

Some flour.

A carton of chicken broth.

Bartles and Jaymes, her adolescent twin brothers, always descended like locusts on the food she brought home with her from her job at the dollar store. At least she got full-time hours now that it was no longer an after-school job. On top of that, she babysat most weekends. But it still wasn't enough money to run the household.

It was their birthday tomorrow, so the twins had left early that morning to go camping for the weekend with their Aunt Bennie and Uncle Josh as a special treat.

Syrah bit her lip. Debra was outdoorsy, back in the day. She used to take the kids camping when Syrah was much younger. Ancient forests surrounded Milbyville. At least some of the moss-draped trees were saplings when the Pilgrims landed on Plymouth

Rock. Wildlife teamed in those old-growth woods, and the eerie sounds the night animals made had kept Syrah awake and cowering in her tent until dawn.

She had felt better, safer, knowing that her mother had been the 4-H Compound Archery champion her junior year in high school, and always had her equipment on the trips. Debra had even taught Syrah and Margarita to shoot a bow and arrow. But that was half a lifetime ago. The only thing Debra shot now was cheap vodka.

Like a surprising number of people in this tiny town, Bennie and Josh were quite well off. They'd paid Debra's mortgage in full the year Chardonnay was born, and kept up with the taxes, since her mother couldn't hold a job for more than a few days. But with each additional child, Debra spiraled further out of control, and the younger kids spent more and more time at their aunt and uncle's home, especially during the school year.

Syrah'd planned to skip dinner, herself. She had to look flawless in the swimsuit leg of the pageant, after all. Truth be told, she had skipped breakfast as well, because there wasn't enough food in the house for everyone, even with Bartles and Jaymes leaving for their trip this morning.

Three 40 oz cans of malt liquor rattled in the door when she opened it. A box of wine took up too much room on the top shelf of the fridge. A single sprouting potato rested on the middle rack and a small, battered container of Brand X powdered milk leaned against one of the sides.

The freezer wasn't any better. There were still a few bags of frozen produce from work that had thawed when that truck hit a utility pole and blacked out four city blocks. Syrah's manager let her have them for free, as long as she promised not to tell anyone. Funny, because she already did a lot of her grocery shopping from items that were supposed to go in the dumpster, anyway. Expiration dates are just guidelines, after all.

She chose a bag of mixed vegetables and set it on the counter. "Chardonnay, would you get me the blender? Boone, I need a saucepan."

Syrah dumped the chickpeas into the blender, along with a splash of vegetable oil and white vinegar to make something hummus-like. She let her sibs eat that with the tortilla chips while she mixed flour, water, a little powdered milk, and the last of the baking soda to make dumplings.

As she stirred the vegetables into the thinned soup, the wicked little Voice in her head started gnawing on her brain, biting off pieces of her soul like a hungry demon. Maybe it *was* a demon for all Syrah knew. It always showed up to kick her when she was down.

How could you even think of abandoning them? You're no better than Debra.

Shut up. Aunt Bennie and Uncle Josh have filed to get custody.

Too bad they didn't care enough about you to do it sooner. Wonder why they waited until you turned 18?

They're doing the best they can. Trying to give me a chance to get out of here. Away from Debra.

Ah, Debra. Whenever she hooked up with some loser, she didn't remember his name, or even to take her birth control pills, but had perfect recall of what she got wasted on. Remembered so well, she named the kid after it. And you inherited that DNA from her. And your dad, whoever he might be. Kind of a lotto, isn't it?

The thought of sharing genetic material with her mother always made her queasy, so she focused on dropping even spoonfuls of dough into the bubbling soup, humming tunelessly to drown out the Voice.

Syrah's stomach growled as she portioned out the soup and dumplings to the smaller children. She put an ice cube in Mogen's to cool it faster. The food smelled so good, and she'd only had a withered apple for lunch.

No. Hunger is the price of freedom. It made her feel skinny, in control. If she could master hunger, she could master anything. She had to win Miss Chicory. First prize was $5,000. Syrah had never seen $5,000 all at once, ever. She wouldn't this time, either. There would be taxes, of course. There were always taxes. But there would be enough for her to move to the city, get a job, and start taking community college classes in the spring.

Miss Chicory may not be nearly as famous as Miss Universe, but something about the Milbyville Fall Festival pageant launched careers. Debra's cousin, Georgia, had won it twenty years ago and moved to Paris to model designer clothes. At least once a year, Aunt Bennie and Uncle Josh jetted off to Europe for a visit.

Syrah'd known the girl who'd won it last year—Mary Anne Shaver. She had moved to New York right after! Sadly, her parents had died in a car crash that same night. They were cremated and the ash-scattering ceremony took place in Vermont, where they'd spent their honeymoon. With no reason for Mary Anne to ever visit her hometown, she and Syrah had lost touch.

Anybody who could get out of Milbyville did... and never looked back.

Syrah was going to be one of those people. Or die trying.

Plastic jack-o'-lanterns clattered as they rolled on the floor. Syrah had been sweeping up during a lull in customers and knocked over the display. It was a week before Halloween and the dollar store was almost sold out of its bargain basement off-brand candy, but decorations still overflowed the shelves.

Should I put some aside, just to make sure the kids have something? The lurid colors on the bags were more off-putting than inviting. Then she remembered that Aunt Bennie would be taking the younger kids trick-or-treating, since they were going to be at her house, anyway.

In that neighborhood? They will make out like bandits.

Syrah smiled at their good fortune as she re-stacked the orange containers. She would be busy being crowned Miss Chicory on Halloween night. Aunt Bennie had promised to come see the pageant after she went out with the kids.

When Syrah got paid on Friday, she planned on going to the outlet mall. Sure, the makeup there was last year's leftovers, but it was good quality. Name-brand. That had to count for something, and she needed any boost available.

She *might* be able to go today. Only she and Margarita would be at the house with Debra tonight. Syrah checked her app to see how much money was in the account. She'd just paid the electric bill, but there had been a little left over.

$1.67.

What? How can that be? There was almost $50 in there! She scrolled down and wanted to scream. A debit for $47.82 from Tom's Discount Liquor.

Last straw achieved. Syrah was 18 now and didn't need to share a bank account with Debra. She would go to the bank first thing in the morning, with her babysitting cash, and open her own account. One that her mother could not access.

She needed to do that, anyway. If Debra got her hands on the money Syrah got from winning Miss Chicory, she'd go on the mother of all benders, and yet again, Syrah would be left with nothing.

Debra slouched at the kitchen table, her heavy head propped on one elbow, when Syrah walked in.

"Debra?"

She opened one eye. "What… d'ya think… you're doing?"

Syrah stood three feet away from her mother, concerned she'd get second-hand intoxication from the alcohol fumes wafting off of her. "Getting home from work. Somebody has to pay the bills."

"Beauty… contesht. Chicory."

"Yes. I entered the contest. And I'm going to win it. Then I'm going to get out of this hellhole."

"No. Forbid it."

Syrah scoffed. "Just watch me."

Debra did not reply. Her head slid off her hand and down her arm, coming to rest on her folded elbow. A wet *grrrnk* spilled out of her mouth.

She didn't even stay awake long enough to ask where the kids were. Syrah stalked to her room, her mother's snores echoing off the tile behind her.

The thrift-shop sewing machine sat on a rickety folding table. The sight of it made Syrah smile. Aunt Bennie had slipped her a hundred dollars toward her pageant clothes. Syrah just needed to put the finishing touches on the dress she'd bought at the same shop and altered for the pageant. The gown was the maroon and white of the radicchio so common on area farms, but she'd covered her pumps in green sequins and crafted a green sequin fascinator, because endive needed love, too.

She'd already completed her modifications to the green swimsuit. She'd found one a few sizes too large, so she had added ruching and beads to simulate the curly leaves of escarole. At the dollar store, she'd lucked onto some barrettes with pale blue aster flowers on them that looked just like wild chicory.

When Syrah finished, she stepped outside into the backyard to practice her routine for the talent phase. She'd been a cheerleader since middle school, so her tumbling skills were strong. Syrah did some warmup stretches and tapped her phone to start the music. She was working to add a fifth back handspring on the last pass. Even if she only had four, she had convinced herself that her routine would rate higher than whatever Kayleigh came up with. That girl had tried out every year and never made the squad.

Syrah purposely avoided looking at the other young women in the dressing room. If they looked prettier than she did, it would make her more nervous than she already was. She knew the Voice would slink out from under its rock and tell her why all the other girls were better than her.

She put on her biggest smile, smoothed her gown, and stepped onto the runway. Syrah heard murmuring in the dark, but the stage lights blinded her to the audience. Just as well. She didn't have to try to imagine them in their underwear.

When she turned back to see Kayleigh waiting in the wings, she almost stopped dead. That girl was a hot mess. Her dress had a wide streak of mud on it, her hair looked like she'd been standing in a wind tunnel, and one of her false eyelashes was missing. She also looked like she was about to burst into tears.

Syrah recoiled at the murderous look Kayleigh flashed at her as the two women passed each other at the curtain.

Is she trying to throw the contest? Why's she mad at me? Syrah hurried to change into her swimsuit.

She was slipping her heels back on when Kayleigh stormed over to her makeup station.

Syrah looked up. "What happened to you?"

"How. Dare. You. Somebody sabotaged my wardrobe and put glue in my hair gel! I wonder who *that* could be?" She stepped forward and Syrah stumbled back, off balance because she was only wearing one heel.

"Ladies!" The stage manager clapped her hands as if they were in elementary school. "Not here. You can beat each other to a pulp after the show, for all I care. But I'm not having this drama right here, right now."

Kayleigh fumed, then stalked back to her own dressing area. Syrah did her turn on the catwalk in her shimmering green swimwear. As Kayleigh passed her, the blue bow on the single strap of her red swimsuit slid down to reveal a safety pin holding the top together. Syrah genuinely felt bad for her, wondering who had wrecked Kayleigh's clothes.

Syrah nailed the fifth handspring in the finale of her routine and got a standing ovation. Kaleigh sang a mediocre, over-played pop song in her mediocre voice.

Back in their evening wear, the women lined up on a riser. The MC stepped to the center stage and gave a speech that dragged on far too long about how wonderful all the contestants were, and how grateful the pageant was to their sponsors, and so on and on and on. Finally, a woman in a black sequined dress walked out on stage and handed him an envelope. He opened it, then smiled and nodded before stretching his arm out to the elegant ladies behind him.

"And now. I'm pleased to announce our second runner-up. Miss Jacqui Cantu!"

Jacqui strutted down the stage to accept her sash and trophy.

"Our first runner-up is Miss Syrah Turner!"

Disappointment flooded over Syrah, and she wanted to flee the stage. She forced her chin up. There was still prize money for second place. She'd make it work, somehow. Syrah marched forward stiffly to be draped with a glittery 'First Runner Up' sash.

The Voice in her head snickered. *That's you. The also-ran. Why did you ever think you could do this?*

"Ladies and gentlemen." He scanned the audience. "This year's queeeeeen of the Harvest Festival, Miss Chicory, is…" He turned and grinned at the pageant contestants. When he faced the audience again, he raised the envelope. "Please give it up for Miss Kayleigh Marrs!"

What? With that filthy dress? The awful hair? The broken makeup? No, no, no, no, no. Were these judges out of their minds? Syrah golf-clapped as Kayleigh made her way to the MC, tears streaming down her cheeks. She gave a saccharine acceptance speech, and they were all dismissed.

Aunt Bennie met her at the stage door. "We got robbed!" She took the clothes-bag from Syrah's hand. "We should go to the judges right now and demand to see the scores. There's no way that—that—I don't know what she is—was better than you. She didn't even come prepared."

Syrah didn't see a point in speaking to the manager. She just wanted to go home and lick her wounds. "Kayleigh did say someone sabotaged her stuff."

"Too bad, so sad. She was not the best. Come on."

Aunt Bennie dragged Syrah to the back office of the venue. The judges were gathering their things, although a couple members of the panel lingered over the marble refreshment table before a set of French doors. They opened out onto a small courtyard at the feet of massive old trees. Gnarled branches cast twisted shadows on the brick pavers from the outside lights. Crickets chirped so loudly their chitinous stylings were nearly as loud indoors as out.

"I want to see the scores," Aunt Bennie snarled at one of the men.

He grinned at her and patted her arm. "Bernadette. You know the judges' decision is final. There's nothing for you here. Not this time."

Sensing danger, everyone else cleared the room.

"That girl did not deserve the title and you know it!"

The man's head tilted. "Don't be greedy. You've had your turn already. Don't you have enough?"

What is he talking about? Cousin Georgia won that pageant ages ago. He didn't seriously think there was any money left from that, did he?

A team of cleaners came in with a cart and cleared off the table in less than a minute, then hurried away. They turned the outside lights off, too.

Something caught Syrah's attention. It took her a minute to figure out what was wrong.

The crickets.

They'd gone silent. Syrah walked toward the French doors as her aunt and the head judge continued their squabble. A mist had risen from the ground. It swirled about a foot off the grass, water droplets reflecting silver-white under the artificial light that shone out through the windows.

Aunt Bennie stopped bickering in mid-sentence. Syrah looked up. Kayleigh shuffled into the room, still in her evening gown, sash and crown. Vacant-eyed and shambling, Syrah half expected her to shout "brains!" and growl.

"Let me take these from you, dear." The judge removed her sash and tiara, then guided her toward the marble table, Aunt Bennie following in his wake.

"No! Not her!" She lunged at Syrah and grabbed her by the shoulders. "She is the best one!"

"Knock it off, Bernadette! Get out of the way." The judge helped Kayleigh lie down on the table and opened the French doors wide. Mist drifted in and lingered above the threshold.

Something dark snaked through the fog. The hair on the back of Syrah's neck prickled, and she tried to move away from the open doors. Aunt Bennie held her fast.

Syrah looked down as a crimson leaf brushed against her ankle. It was attached to a dark vine that slithered across the rug. She hopped to the side, away from it. Aunt Bennie shoved her back toward the thing.

"Get away from her!"

Syrah's head snapped toward her mother's voice in the doorway.

Debra leaned against the doorframe, nocking an arrow. "I should have done this years ago. How could you do that to Georgia? Your own daughter? Always wondered why you visited, but never had any pictures with her. Why all the Miss Chicories went on tour or moved away the minute they won. And then I found out. I saw…"

Her voice broke and she swallowed hard. "I saw what happened to those girls. That thing almost got me, too. Sometimes, I wish it had. Can't get it out of my head. And you knew. You knew what was going to happen to Georgia, and you let that monster take her. For money."

Debra let the arrow fly, but her hands shook and it hit Bernadette in the shoulder.

"You crazy bitch!" Bennie shouted as she let go of Syrah.

The black vine veered and twined up her leg with horrifying speed, twisting around her waist and throat. Bennie clawed at it with both hands as she gasped for air. It jerked her leg out from under her and she fell hard. Gurgling and choking, she disappeared into the blanket of mist.

Christmas fell a bit late this year. Debra had spent ninety days in a residential re-hab to get dried out. In January, she came home to a McMansion in the suburbs of a comfortably large city. Far from the ancient trees and the arcane creatures that lived among them. Location didn't seem to matter. They'd left Milbyville far behind, and still the money followed them.

Aunt Bennie seemed like a small sacrifice to make.

TOWNSENDE & HARDWICKE: HOUNDED

By Artemis Greenleaf

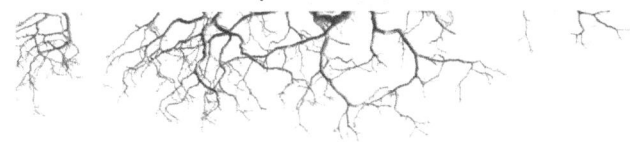

KINGSLEY Hardwicke pulled his damp cloak tighter around his neck. The icy wind cut through the woolen garment like frozen blades, setting his teeth chattering.

"How much farther?" Algar Townsende swept his shaggy blond hair out of his eyes and rubbed his arms.

Kingsley dodged a puddle in the rutted, muddy road. "Still a fair way. I fear we shall arrive at the abbey later than our errand demands."

"Pity we lost the horses. We would already be sat down to supper with the Abbot, were we bestride."

"So it is. I reckon the bell for vespers has long been rung, but surely we shall arrive ere the start of the compline."

Algar kicked a rock, but stumbled as the sucking mud held it fast. "Ye gods. Of all days to be far from a locked door at sunset."

"We are in the countryside, my friend. There may yet be a quaint bonfire to warm us this Allhallond Evening."

"The countryside of East Anglia. Perhaps you forget that Æthelwold, the roguish Dane, still seeks to rouse the rabble against his cousin, King Edward. If we were taken as spies, it would go ill for us. And worse were we forced into his army. Nay, I do not care to tarry, even at the brightest fire."

A stick snapped in the woods to their right, and both men reached for their sword hilts as they whirled toward the noise. Long afternoon shadows seeped across the road, pooling under the trees, where the gloom rivaled that of night.

Kingsley pushed aside the leather thong that held his blade in its scabbard. "What ho, good sir or madam. Show yourself! We mean you no harm, but we are none to be trifled with."

No answer came from the darkling wood. The tall undergrowth rippled, as if someone, bent low to the ground, hurried away from them.

"A fox, most like." Algar released his grip on the weapon.

"Perhaps. Still, we should be on our guard."

Helios rimmed the puddles with pink and orange as he slipped below the horizon. Misty twilight shrouded the road ahead.

Algar craned his neck. "Oi, on yon hillock. Mayhap that light is the abbey?"

"Aye, and no more than half a league distant, by my reckoning. We shall be there afore the abbot tucks up in his bed." Kingsley's jaw relaxed as now their goal seemed within reach.

"The feast day of All Saints is on the morrow. I'll wager his bed lays empty tonight."

The mud squished and slurped under their boots as they tramped along. Kingsley frowned, thinking he heard another set of feet slopping along with them. He stopped, raising his hand to signal Algar to do the same.

The wet patter also halted. Holding his breath, Kingsley slowly turned to look over his shoulder.

Algar swore and flailed his hand at his weapon, missing it in his panic.

A black dog-shaped miscreation the size of a bull stood behind them, veiled in a sickly green glimmer. The monster's slavering lips parted, revealing three rows of jagged teeth. Its eyes shone like molten iron, casting a reddish glow across its fearsome features.

Kingsley snatched Algar's arm. "It's the Black Shuck. A harbinger of doom. And whether it be of the faery realm or made by the Devil himself, you cannot harm it."

Algar's hand finally alighted on the heft of his blade and drew it from its sheath. "Fie! I can and I shall!"

"No!" Kingsley grabbed his companion around the waist. "It is not a thing of flesh. To hinder it is to invite disaster. Prithee stay your hand, Algar. Put away your steel. You shall send us both to perdition if you cross it."

The beast stood like a basalt carving, malice rolling off it in waves. And yet it made no move to savage them.

Panting, Algar lowered his blade. The Shuck's upper lip curled, but it made no other move. Kingsley turned his friend by his elbow to face the distant abbey. "Be calm and steady. Ignore it as best you can."

Algar did not resheath his sword, and Kingsley governed his rash companion by keeping a tight hold on his arm, each jarring step a prayer that the beast did not fall upon them and devour their souls. Kingsley's blood pounded in his ears, mercifully drowning out the footfalls of the grotesque creature behind them. They had legged about half the distance to the abbey when he glanced over his shoulder. The Black Shuck was gone. Kingsley knew not whence and wished it good riddance.

He loosened his grip on his friend and let the stagnant air from his lungs. "We have lost our not-so-amiable companion."

Bells tolled ahead. "The call to colliato, I'll warrant."

Algar's stomach growled. "Let us hope they saved us some bread."

"And their most excellent mead."

"Huzzah!"

"I'm glad our brush with fate has not dulled your appetite."

The road sloped downward and meandered through a copse of trees, darkening suddenly. Kingsley paused, drawing his own sword. "Be on your guard. This narrows may be a robber's den."

Algar nodded, clutching his hilt. The two men cautiously trod through the gloom. They relaxed when they reached the other side with no mishap.

But their relief was short-lived.

Four brigands melted out of the trees and blocked their way. "What ho!" called the tallest. "I believe you have my purse, good sir. Hand it over."

Kingsley stiffened, calculating their odds against the band of thieves. He and Algar were both seasoned soldiers, but age and battle scars had taken their toll. In the deepening twilight, even the smallest of the four was half a head taller than he.

The pack he carried contained letters and monies from the bishop, and a holy relic for the foundation of a new cathedral.

"Come on then! Hand us over your purse, or we'll send you to the Devil."

Algar stepped closer to Kingsley so the two were shoulder to shoulder. He raised his sword. "In the words of Leonidas, come and take it."

The bandits circled them and their leader swung his double handed claymore at Algar's head. The smaller man parried, but his own sword was nearly knocked from his hands by the force of the blow.

Now back-to-back, Algar and Kingsley slowly pinwheeled at the center as the robbers stalked a circle around them. Kingsley planned to feint at the footpad to his right, then go for the boss, who glowered in front of him.

Before he could move, the leader violently leaned to his left and the man closest to him lunged to his right. Their heads crashed together with a sickening crunch. As they crumpled to the ground, the other two turned tail and fled to the forest.

A figure loomed over the fallen highwaymen, barely discernable in the murk. "*Dia duit.* Ya well, then? God's body, is that Townsende and Hardwicke?"

He speaks the tongue of the Celts. Kingsley peered into the dark but could make out precious few details about the stranger. "Gramercy, good sir, for our salvation. But you have us at a disadvantage. You ken our names and I fain would know yours."

"Conchar McKays, I am entitled. But I mostly am called Kays."

"We've business with the abbot, Kays. Would you—"

"He's the one sent me after you, ain't he?"

"Rathe, then. We wish to speak to him afore he takes his bed." Algar planted his hands on his hips.

The stranger snorted. "On this night? Nay, he keeps the vigil for the dead until matins. They creep from their graves to visit their old homes. Must return to the churchyard by cock crew. But the good angels have blessed you. Tomorrow is the Feast Day of Allhallonds." He rubbed his palms together. "The cooks have already begun their merry business."

What codswallop! Dead is dead—there's no comin' back. God knows I've seen enough of it. Kingsley bit his tongue. A gust of air tugged at his cloak and a few gelid raindrops fell on his face. He shivered.

"Best move our shanks. Storm's comin'." Kays started down the lane.

The trio strode apace through the benighted village, the tall Celt leading the way to Fulbourn Abbey.

The wind picked up, howling around them. They almost made it to the monastery before the bottom fell out of the sky and the gale drove horizontal pellets of rain against their faces.

At least there's a portico. Kingsley and Algar squeezed water from their cloaks as they waited for someone to let them in after Kays' urgent knocking.

After a time, the spyhole cover was pulled back and a pale visage peered through the iron grating.

"Let us in, Brother Cedric!" boomed Kays.

Torches in wall sconces nearly flickered out in the wind that roared in at the opening of the silent door. The soggy travelers stepped inside to drip on the flagstone floor.

The three stood before a bony monk, his face sour as old vinegar. "Are you certain these are the right carles? They wear no battle-sark."

Kays' lips tightened. "Go and fetch the abbot."

Cedric harumphed and strode away.

Kays hung their sodden cloaks near the fireplace and set off to find dry clothes. Kingsley and Algar stripped off their mail-coats, made all the heavier by the soaked fabric. The rows of iron rings sewn onto them had been oiled to prevent rust, and Kingsley hoped it was enough. By the time the round and jovial abbot appeared, Cedric in his wake, Kays, Algar, and Kingsley were all dressed in the rough brown tunics of the monks.

"Greetings, Reverend Father Fairchilde. Kingsley Hardwicke and my companion, Algar Townsende, at your service."

The travelers each gave a slight bow.

Fairchilde waved his hand. "Now, now. No need for that. Have you the box?"

Kingsley retrieved a strongbox from his soggy pack and handed it over.

"Key?" Fairchilde raised his eyebrows.

Outside, the wind screamed around the corners like an angry banshee and rain pelted so fiercely against the shutters it nearly drowned the abbot's words.

Algar pulled a fine iron chain from around his neck. A brass key that ended in a triskelion with an emerald at its center dangled from the links. "Reverend Father."

The abbot took it and opened the box. He skipped over the bulging pouch of gold and the wax-sealed letters to a linen bag about the length of Kingsley's hand and half as wide. Fairchilde handed the box off to Cedric and withdrew a blackened chunk of wood. He pressed it to his forehead, then kissed it reverently.

Cedric leaned forward, trying to get a better look in the dim lobby. "Is it...?"

Fairchilde nodded. "Yes. A piece of the one true cross."

Kingsley raised a skeptical eyebrow but said nothing. The bishop had sent it, so it wasn't within the scope of Kingsley's employ to confirm or deny its authenticity.

Pursing his thin lips, Cedrick turned to Kingsley. "Well, then. You've delivered the strongbox. It is forbidden for the uninitiated to stay overnight within these walls, thus I bid you a good evening."

"What!" Kays snorted. "You would send these brave souls out into this storm, on Allhallonds Evening no less, without even a bite of supper for all their trouble?"

The abbot slipped the relic back into its pouch. "Of course you will shelter here! As few pilgrims trek this way, our hostelry is small, but I would not think to send you into the tempest. Kays, show them to the refectory. Brother Cedric, seek brother Adil in the kitchen and ask him to bring supper to our guests."

With that, the abbot hurried away. Kays, Cedric, Kingsley, and Algar walked until they reached the end of the corridor and were obliged to turn to the left. Cedric unlocked an iron-bound oaken door and relocked it when the group passed through. Russet-painted doors faced each other on opposite sides of the hallway, two on each side.

"This is the hostelry," Cedric muttered.

Kingsley scarce caught the words, but the monk stopped not, so he assumed the sleeping arrangements would be dealt with after supper. He wondered if the last visitors had been gone long enough for the fleas to have given up hope of a warm body and abandoned the bedclothes.

They passed through another portal, this one unlocked. The plain wood doors of monks' cells lined both sides of the corridor. An open archway led to the refectory, with tables and benches aplenty.

"Seat yourselves. I'll speak to the brothers in the kitchen." Cedric and Kays continued through the dining hall without them.

Algar and Kingsley's stomachs growled in unison. The scents of fresh baked bread and roasted meats still lingered from an earlier meal. Rich aromas of butter and herbs wafted through the archway from the kitchen. The murmur of quiet voices was punctuated by the sounds of food being prepared.

They sat at the nearest table and Kingsley winced. He'd been on his feet for so long that once his weight was removed, they ached all the way up to his knees. He wondered if Algar felt the same road weariness.

"I could sleep the sleep of the dead, and that anon." Kingsley stretched his long legs under the table.

"Hush! You mustn't speak of such things, especially not tonight, and with the churchyard but a stone's throw. Who knows what shades are about?"

Kingsley was saved from a reply by Kays, with beakers of mead, and a monk sweeping in with trays of food: most of a loaf of bread, mussels cooked with leeks, roasted root vegetables, mushroom soup, and an ox tongue with a red sauce. Hunger riveted his gaze on the victuals, but when he raised his eyes to thank the monk, his jaw gaped open.

"A moor!"

Brother Adil gave a small nod as he set the food on the table and gave Algar and Kingsley each a wooden trencher.

Algar tore off a thick chunk of bread. "Forgive my companion's rudeness, Brother. He can be a harecop at times."

Kingley's nostrils flared as he shot a hard glance at Algar before focusing on the monk. "Yes, forgive me, Brother. I meant no offense."

"Think no more on it. I am a long way from Córdoba." He smiled before he turned away for the kitchen.

Kays gave them each a cup. "I shall leave you to your meal. I've work yet to do this evening."

The two travelers fell upon the food like ravenous wolves. A short time later, Algar cried out.

"What is it?" Kingsley whipped his head around, scanning the room. "Are you hurt?"

"This sauce! It is cool to the touch, and yet it burns my mouth!"

Kingsley chuckled. "I have heard of this. It is called Saracen's Sauce. Just the thing to make a bland ox tongue palatable."

They continued their predations until their bellies threatened to overflow. Kingsley yawned. "I would lay my head down. Should we seek the hostelry?"

"Follow me." Brother Cedric stepped from the doorway, where he must have secreted himself until they were done with their feast.

They arose and trailed him down the corridor. Cedric indicated that they were to take the two rooms closest to the locked door, one on each side of the hall.

"Rest ye well for your travels tomorrow. But do not for any reason, save the direst of need, leave your rooms until you are sent for on the morrow."

Algar's jaw trembled as he attempted to stifle a yawn. "Thank you, Brother. And a good night to you."

"Goodnight, Brother Cedric."

The churlish monk turned on his heel and hurried away.

Kingsley shook his head as he opened the reddish door. The chamber was spartan—not unlike a monk's cell—furnished with a narrow bed on one wall and a writing desk and chair at the end of the narrow room, underneath a window.

It was missing a single item, but a vitally important one. "Gah, where's the chamber pot?"

There was none to be found, and his need grew greater by the moment. *This seems a dire enough circumstance.* He opened his door and stepped into the corridor, hoping to either find a monk to assist him, or a door to the bailey so he could irrigate the shrubbery. The hallway was deserted as he strode toward the refectory. He'd remembered seeing a door to the outside there.

Kingsley burst into the grassy courtyard, overjoyed that the rain had let up, and hiked his tunic to relieve himself, and not a moment too soon.

As he dropped the hem of the tunic, someone cleared their throat behind him. Shame burned his cheeks. He hadn't noticed anyone out in the garden, but it was mostly dark. There were few torches lit in the refectory at this time to shed their light on the bailey.

Sheepish, he turned around. "Forgive me, Brother. My need was great, and there—" Kingsley's tongue froze in his mouth.

The monk facing him was half again his own height. And from the cowl peeked not the face of a man, but a mastiff dog. *What kind of mushrooms were in that soup?*

"I am Brother Bartholomew." The monk lowered his cowl, revealing floppy ears and a thick neck. His fur thinned the closer it got to the collar of his tunic.

"Brother…? Kings… I'm Kingsley."

"Fear not, Kingsley. I mean you no harm. I abandoned the fierce ways of my people long ago, and I have been welcomed at Fulbourn Abbey for many a year. But I ken that few men have encountered the Kynokephaloi and lived to tell the tale."

As Kingsley struggled to bring his numb tongue to life, a white reptilian head peeked from Bartholomew's tunic.

"Easy, Baldric. This carle is no foe."

The creature squirmed its way out of the monk's tunic. He boosted it onto his shoulder, where it stood on its two legs and unfurled pale green batlike wings.

Kingsley blinked rapidly, but the small beast was there every time he opened his eyes. "You have a wyvern named Baldric?"

"Yes. He's just a baby." Bartholomew frowned. "His mother was slaughtered by some beef-witted atheling."

A gust of wind shook the apple tree above Kingsley, scattering chilly droplets on his head and shoulders.

"Come inside. I shall equip you for the night so you don't drown our orchard."

The traveler followed the giant monk into the abbey. Bartholomew retrieved a bucket for him and sent him back to the hostelry. He feared his bizarre encounter would keep him awake, but as soon as he pulled the woolen blanket up to his neck, Morpheus opened wide his arms to welcome him.

Kingsley dreamed of chortling monks but could not discern the source of their mirth. Gradually, he became aware of men shouting. He thought at first it was part of his dream, but he rose from the abyss of sleep like a stork taking to the sky. Pounding came at his door and he threw off his covers, grubbling through the stygian gloom to answer it.

"Rathe! Rathe!" Algar gesticulated wildly.

"What—"

"Cedric has been slain!"

Kingsley grabbled his brand in its scabbard, buckling it over his monk's robe as he hurried after Algar to the refectory.

A score or more brothers stood in a loose circle. Some had clasped their hands together and breathed hushed prayers. Others, disquieted by the evil turn of events, stood with mouths agape. They parted silently as Kingsley and Algar approached.

Dim torchlight revealed the horror. Algar's hand flew to his mouth, and Kingsley had scarce seen such carnage since last he was upon the battlefield. Brother Cedric's body had been reaved of its head, and the gore-smeared orb lay some feet away. Both arms had parted company with their shoulders and lay bent at angles, one underneath the corpse, the other on a table where it had been flung. Poor Cedric's belly had been split like a ripe melon, his offal spread around him and partly devoured.

Kingsley's mind strayed to the Black Shuck that had trailed them earlier as he studied the grisly tableau. *Was it a* harbinger *of this death, or its* author? "Where is the abbot?"

A nearby monk replied, "He fainted dead away when he espied this grewsome murder of Brother Cedric. He was carried to his rooms."

Algar stroked his beard. "Who found him thus?"

An uncanny monk lowered his cowl. "Who has given you leave to ask questions? We ne'er had such slaughter afore your arrival."

The whispered prayers ceased as all eyes fell on Kingsley and Algar.

Heavy footfalls sounded on the stone floor. Brother Bartholomew ducked low and entered the refectory from the archway that led to the kitchen. "Brother Zoricus, this is a discussion for Reverend Father Fairchilde, is it not? You impugn our guests, and yet they are messengers from Bishop de Biville himself. Do you reckon he would truck with murderers?"

Zoricus drew up his cowl, hiding his unlovely features. "Perhaps not, Bartholomew. But the fact remains that this wanton slaughter was visited upon us the night of their arrival."

The debate continued as Algar tugged at Kingsley's sleeve. "Am I mad? Or does the snout of a hound protrude from the giant's cowl?"

Kingsley turned his head to whisper. "Indeed it does."

"A healfhundinga?"

"He told me he was of the Kynokephaloi people, though I confess I thought he and Baldric walked only through my dreams."

"Baldric? Another of his kind?"

"Nay. A wyvern bairn."

"By God's own bones! A dragonlet, too. Are not the dog-heads infamous for their lust of human flesh?"

"He has renounced those ways, or so he confided to me."

"Mayhap, but he is a fearsome thing."

Bartholomew cleared his throat. "Then let us take this matter to the abbot, Zoricus." He gestured toward Kingsley and Algar.

Brother Adil stepped in front of a group of monks who had moved behind Zoricus. "We should prepare our brother for his long repose. Brother Caroc, kindly fetch a sheet of linen for his shroud."

Zoricus, Bartholomew, Kingsley, and Algar made their way down the corridor to the abbot's rooms. When they arrived, his door was open. He sat at a table with a mug. Two monks spoke with him in low tones.

"Reverend Father!" called Zoricus. "Are you well?"

The abbot turned to the small fellowship at his door. "Yes, I am much recovered, thanks to Brother Cassius and his herb craft. I have been praying for our Brother Cedric."

"Prayers are well, Reverend Father." Bartholomew bowed his great head slightly. "But we must call a moot. Whoever has joined Cain's transgression must be found out and justice served."

Zoricus scoffed. "No such council is necessary. The murderer is in this room."

Fairchilde stiffened. "Is he? And who would you lay charges against?"

"We never had such foul deeds until these two carles arrived." His lip jerked into a momentary sneer. "They claim to be sent by the bishop, and yet they are not weeded as warriors for such a perilous journey. Perhaps Brother Cedric caught them sneak-thieving and they silenced him."

The abbot raised an eyebrow. "And yet the same could be said of you, Brother Zoricus. Perhaps you made to steal the treasure they had ferried to me, and Brother Cedric intercepted your vile plot. It beseems you are quick to point your finger."

The monk spluttered. "I would never!"

"Then throw not harsh accusations against others, unless you have proof of their merit."

Chastised, Zoricus bowed his head.

Fairchilde turned to Brother Bartholomew. "Did you see aught last eventide?"

"Not but Hardwicke in the bailey."

"The bailey you say!"

"There was no chamber pot," Kingsley hung his head.

The abbot pursed his lips and crossed his arms.

Algar glanced around the room. "Where is Kays? He had labors still when we parted. Mayhap he witnessed a stranger?"

Fairchilde shook his head. "Nay. He returned to his home in the village once his milking was complete. Brother Cedric was with me in the cloister when Kays brought in his buckets. He shall return with the sun."

Kingsley ran a hand through his grizzled hair. "Reverend Father, let us conference together to suss out the murderer."

The abbot chewed the inside of his cheek, then nodded. "Yes. More heads are better than one in such a case." He dismissed the two monks who had been tending to him.

"Did Brother Cedric have any family? At least they should receive the weregild." Algar looked from Fairchilde to Zoricus.

"If he did, I am not aware. He was left here as a child and none e'er came to claim him." The abbot shook his head.

Zoricus shrugged.

Mayhap that explains some of his bitterness. "Zoricus, please favor us with your account of finding Brother Cedric."

Zoricus cast his eyes to the abbot, who nodded. "After nocturns, I betook myself to the scriptorium to read. I wished to speak with Brother Adil, so I hied myself to the kitchen."

"Was he there?" Kingsley asked.

"Nay." Zoricus lowered his eyes and shook his head. "All the cooks had already taken to their beds for a sleep before matins." His voice lowered. "There was a loaf end, and I thought to get myself some soup and sop it with the bread. That is how I came to be in the refectory."

Algar stifled a yawn. "Was Brother Cedric at nocturns?"

"I cannot be certain. The air was chill and all of the brothers had their cowls up."

Kingsley turned to Fairchilde. "After we went to sup, whence did you go?"

"To my quarters and stowed the strongbox in a chest and locked it down. Thereafter, I betook myself to the cloister. I spoke with Brother Cedric, Brother Nicodemus, and Brother Favian with regards to the feasting on this day. After Kays brought in his pails, I repaired to the church with Brother Nicodemus to attend to the vigil for the dead. When Brother Sadon and Brother Ulric arrived to spell us, I took to my bedchamber. I was too weary to endure more."

"Did you go immediately to sleep?"

"I did. Brother Zoricus woke me after finding Brother Cedric."

"Is there any avenue wherein someone could attain the refectory from outside the abbey?"

"No. E'en the chapter house is secured."

Algar shifted his weight. "Do you know of the Black Shuck? Some say it is fell and reckless and could tear a man asunder."

Fairchilde's eyes narrowed. "The Devil's dog could not set its paw on hallowed ground."

I wonder. "Did Brother Cedric have enemies? Had he words with any brother? Was there aught who would cherish a grudge against him?"

"Alas, Brother Cedric was less than blithesome. Yet even in his churlishness, he had no quarrel with any man."

Algar's eyes widened, and he drew in a deep breath. "You say Brother Cedric was a foundling. Could he be a bastard son of the erstwhile King Alfred? It would be in the interest of both King Edward and his challenger, Æthelwold, to dispatch any contenders to the throne."

"If that is his lineage, I have no ken of it."

Kingsley bit his lip. "I hate to ask it, for Brother Bartholomew has been naught but kind, but has he e're displayed fits of temper?"

A church bell tolled.

"That is the call to matins. Nay, Brother Bartholomew is the soul of patience. Fearsome as he may appear, he is docile as a lamb." Fairchilde outstretched his hands. "I bid you stay the day. Feast with us. You are battle tested; we are not hard men. Would you stay the night and keep watch? Surely the bishop will not find fault if you tarry with us in this matter."

"Of course we will aid you, Reverend Father." Kingsley bowed.

Kingsley rubbed sleep from his eyes. Even after his nap, his belly was uncomfortably full.

"I feel crapulous." Algar groaned.

"A few rounds of the abbey should sort it out."

They had traded in their borrowed monk's tunics for their own dry clothes and girded themselves with both sword and dirk. The abbey was laid out like a blocky figure of eight. The lobby, hostelry, and bailey garden at one end, the cloister, chapter house, and church at the other. After two circuits of patrol, they had sighted no interloper.

On their third round, they had just entered the scriptorium when the hairs on the back of Kingsley's neck did uprise. He halted.

A lone torch flickered in a sconce, casting most of the large room into darkness.

Dread gripped Kingsley's insides with an cyle hand as he sniffed the air. "Do you smell that?"

Algar also raised his nose. "A beast of some sort. It reeks of rotting meat and piss."

"Our killer is at hand, I ween."

Both men drew their weapons, heads on a swivel, seeking any movement in the gloom. Manic giggling erupted from the blackness and bounced off the stone walls and floor.

Algar squinted. "Not a beast? A man who's lost his wits?"

The frantic laughter came again. Something moved in the dark. A foul thing stepped from behind a table, its eyes glowing green. It approached the circle of light, its maw agape, shewing its wicked teeth. The scruffy, tawny coat was blotched with brown spots and its forelimbs were longer than the hind. It let out a shuddering growl that sent rivers of ice down Kingsley's spine.

"What the Devil is that?" Algar edged closer to Kingsley.

"Neither Shuck nor Kynokephaloi. I'll wager it weighs ten stone if it weighs a pound. But from whence it has been conjured I cannot guess."

As one, they took a step toward the monster. It raised its brutish head, then trotted away down the corridor. They followed swift behind, hoping to catch it at the locked door between the lobby and the hostelry, but they could find neither hide nor hair of the thing, though they sought it the rest of the night, even after the monks arose and began their nocturns at the strike of three.

When those offices were completed at five, the abbot called all the monks together to hear what Kingsley and Algar had found. They described the monster they'd seen in the scriptorium.

Brother Adil pulled down his cowl. "I know this beast. It is cunning and strong, but it is merely an animal. It is called a hyena and must have escaped from the earl's menagerie."

"Are you sure?" asked the abbot. "That estate is some distance away."

"Hyena can run for hours. They are as curious as they are fierce."

Fairchilde nodded. "Then I shall send Kays to Wandlebury to ask the earl to retrieve his pet at once."

Dinner was a pleasant memory. Kingsley and Algar prepared to take to the road when Kays returned.

The abbot peered over his shoulder, as if seeking travelers further down the road. "Well? What says the earl?"

"Reverend Father, he sends his condolences on our loss of Brother Cedric. But he had ne'er heard tell of a hyena, and reckoned we should seek it in the fens."

"That is ill news indeed." Fairchilde stroked his white beard.

"Algar and myself will hunt the thing. If we find it not before sundown, we shall strive to intercept the beast should it attempt to return to the abbey."

They put on their mailcoats, bent on the destruction of the hateful creature. By sunset, they were sheathed in stinking mud, but no closer to capturing the animal. They set themselves upon the road to the abbey, and it was full dark when they arrived. A weary night's patrol yielded no hyena.

"Mayhap it is gone." Algar leaned against the wall.

The front door to the abbey opened and Brother Bartholomew beckoned to them. "The beast hath returned and taken Brother Caroc with it."

"God's bones! It came not from outside. It must be secreted within," Kingsley cried.

The two old soldiers followed Bartholomew inside to assist with the sad business of tending Caroc's scattered remains. At dinner, the brothers had little appetite, though Kingsley and Algar were famished and ate heartily.

Brother Adil beckoned to them from the kitchen when their trenchers were empty. They went to him, and he pulled them away from the doorway so they might not be observed.

"What news have you, Brother Adil?" Algar wiped his mouth on his sleeve.

"I fear this is no natural hyena, but a stick man."

Kingsley's brow furrowed. "Do tell."

"A stick man is a were-hyena. He rubs an accursed stick upon his body after the setting of the sun and thus he transforms into a ravening beast."

"The stick. What is its like?"

"A sorcerer could avail his evil magic upon any scrap of wood."

"Would the carle remember what he has done in animal form?" Algar asked.

"I know not."

"Then let us find out. Come, Algar." Kingsley strode down the corridor.

"Whither do we go?" Algar jogged to catch up.

"Follow me and say nothing."

Kingsley rapped upon the door and waited. Thrice he knocked, but there came no reply. Trying the handle, he found it unlatched and began to push the door open.

"We cannot enter the abbot's private quarters unbidden!"

"I'll warrant forgiveness is better sought than permission on this errand."

The two men slipped into the empty chamber. Three fat candles burned on a table, adding to the flickering light from the dying blaze in the great fireplace. A chest had been thrown open, and the strongbox they had delivered lay on the bed, still containing its gold and missives.

"Look for the relic, Algar."

"The holy cross? That cannot be!"

"I fear it is."

They ransacked the room but found aught. Kingsley inhaled sharply through his nostrils twice and raised his hand. "Harken!"

"I hear no—"

A tawny blur leaped at Algar, knocking him to the floor. The were-hyena stood on his chest, slaver dripping on Algar's face.

Kingsley drew his sword and slashed, the blade bouncing back as if the monster were made of stone. He pummeled its head with the hilt of his sword, but it turned to him and pulled back its lips into a savage rictus. Even as he distracted the beast, he noted Algar's hand stretch forth toward the chamber pot.

I'm near o'erwhelmed by this devil dog's stench already. But lo, Algar had found the relic, lain careless behind the bucket. He tossed it wildly toward Kingsley. It slipped through his outstretched fingers and skittered across the floor.

The creature turned on Kingsley and clamped its vicious jaws on his wrist. He cried out as he felt the bones would surely break under such assault. Algar scrambled to his feet, ran around his embattled friend and snatched up the wooden talisman.

The were-hyena leapt at him as he tossed it into the fire. Once it took on the flames, the monster let out a prodigious roar. It flailed on the floor, moaning and laughing, switching form betwixt abbot and hyena as rapid as the blinking of an eye.

When the wood was thence consumed, the sweat-soaked abbot lay senseless upon the flagstone. While Kingsley bound his wound with a leg of the abbot's hose, Algar slapped the prelate's cheeks and tweaked his nose until his eyes fluttered open.

"Awake, Reverend Father. The beast has been dispatched."

Fairchilde sat up. "You have slain it?"

Kingsley hid his wounded arm behind his back. "It will trouble you no more. Shall we repair to the kitchen? I lange for some roasted meat."

SIDE QUEST

By A. B. Richards

Dennis "Dingo" Durham grinned into the camera. "G'day, Monster Mob. Glad you could rock up to our third annual live Halloween show. Six hours of nuts-and-bolts monster hunting. All the mozzie-slapping goodness that is a live expedition. So, buckle up, Mobsters, it's gonna be a ripper."

The camera panned the location. Television series team members, Julie—the tech specialist, Marquis—the psychic, and Salvador—the cofounder of Monster Busters, each waved as they came into frame. A dark forest of tall pines loomed behind them.

Salvador gestured to someone off camera, and a young woman with hot pink hair joined him. "This is Mozelle. She won the contest to join us live tonight."

"Hi. It's so amazing to be here." Mozelle stepped back and two young men came into frame, one wiry and the other well-fed.

Salvador shook their hands. "And of course, you guys have met our friends, Shag and Mickey, from East Tex Paranormal. Let's bust some monsters."

The image jiggled slightly as the camera operator began following the team up the trail.

Dingo opened his arms to the shadowy trees. "We're here in the Sam Houston National Forest to meet Jim Saddler, who claims he had a dogman encounter when he was camping by the lake two months ago. He spent a night of terror as something wrecked his campsite and pawed at his tent." He made claws of his hands and scraped the air for emphasis.

Julie turned her face to the camera. "Since we are live, we don't have the fancy graphics and animations like our usual weekly show. If you're not familiar with the dogman creature, think Bigfoot, except with a wolf's head. And it can run on all fours. They're reported to be anywhere from six to ten feet tall. Some people say it's a werewolf, or even a skinwalker, and others that it's a species of cryptid, and not in any way human. Who knows? Maybe werewolves and dogmen are two similar but distinct creatures. Also, like Bigfoot, lots of people report seeing them, but no bodies have ever been recovered."

Salvador jogged into view. "We plan to take a little side quest and leave here around 1 AM to head over and try and catch the Bragg Road lights. There have also been Bigfoot sightings in the area, so we may get double lucky. It's a drive, but you can grab a snack and eat with us on the trip."

Sounds of night animals accompanied them down the trail. The cameras caught occasional eye shine as curious critters investigated the media parade before fleeing into the brush. Light from the waning gibbous moon reflected off the lake ahead.

As they came out of the trees, they turned right. A four-person tent, the type tall enough for most people to stand up inside, had been pitched near the shore. A lantern glowed through the plastic windows. Another lantern sat on a folding table between a group of camp chairs. A fire pit blazed a few yards from the tent, and a man with a koozie-clad can was silhouetted against the flames.

Dingo quickened his pace, reaching out toward the figure. "Jim? Thanks for contacting Monster Busters."

Jim shook Dingo's hand. He was young—late twenties to early thirties—and generically good-looking. He glanced over his shoulder toward the tree line. "Thanks for coming out."

Salvador and Julie seated themselves on either side of Dingo and Jim in front of the fire. Marquis made his way to the tent and sat in one of the camp chairs, eyes closed. The others milled around the campsite.

Dingo patted Jim on the shoulder. "Alright, mate. Tell us your story."

Jim raised the can to his lips and took a swig. "Well, it was a Thursday night. July 27. I like to camp during the week—less crowded. Anyway. I had been hiking all day and already eaten my dinner. I was pretty tired, but I was laying on my cot reading a book."

"Sounds delightful!" Julie chirped.

"Yeah, it was. Until I heard two men talking. Not enough to understand what they said, just deep voices going back and forth."

"Is that normal for this campground? Would there be other hikers out at night?" Dingo slapped at a bug.

"Well. The park was at least half full, so there were a lot of people around. That's why I usually stick to the primitive sites, like this one. Less traffic. A raccoon was trilling and chattering as it hunted at the edge of the lake. And owls. Screech owls are real creepy—sound like little UFOs. Anyway, soon as those guys quit talking, everything went quiet. There was not a sound. I thought I might have gone deaf suddenly, like a stroke or something, so I smacked my leg to make some noise. I definitely heard that, so I knew it wasn't me."

Dingo nodded. "They call that the Oz Effect here in paranormal circles. Not sure if hunters have a name for it, but when that happens, they say it means a large predator is in the area. Is that what you felt, Jim?"

"Yeah. I definitely felt like I was being watched. I looked out the windows but didn't see anything. Not at first."

Salvador leaned forward. "When *did* you see it?"

"Them. There were at least two. My tent is six and a half feet tall. When I looked out, something dark and hairy ran by. It was chest level with the window. I'm guessing it was somewhere between seven and eight foot tall. I turned around, and another one was looking at me. Had a wolf's face and glowing red eyes. Folks may call me crazy, but I know what I saw."

"The Monster Busters believe you, Jim." Dingo grinned and rested a hand on the hapless camper's shoulder.

"Thank you. But all of that, that's not even the worst part. They threw all of my stuff around, broke my $400 cooler, shredded both my camp chairs, and then they would drag their claws along the sides of my tent from time to time. Like they were trying to say, 'We know you're in there and we can get you any time we want.' I pulled the blanket over my head and held my .22."

"Why didn't you shoot at them, mate?"

"If you'd seen the size of those things, you'd see how it would just piss them off. I thought if I didn't antagonize them, they'd get bored and go away. I mean, the head of the one that looked in the window is like the size of your torso."

"That's a big fella." Dingo got to his feet. "Now show us where *she* was."

Jim exhaled deeply and slowly rose. Reluctantly, he walked toward the trees. "It was almost dawn, according to my watch. The noise outside had stopped. Then there was this voice. Like my sister's, but not quite. It's hard to explain. But it was almost like there was another voice underneath hers, ever so slightly out of sync. I looked out the window and saw her standing there." He pointed to a large oak.

Julie's brow furrowed. "Would your sister come out here to visit you?"

Jim bowed his head. "No. She died two years ago."

"I'm so sorry."

"Thank you." Jim swallowed hard. "She raised her arm, beckoning for me to come out there. But I knew if I did, it would be the last thing I would ever do."

The Monster Busters spent the next two and a half hours scanning the forest with FLIR cameras, attempting EVP sessions, and trying to provoke the dogmen to come out. The most nefarious creature they encountered was a 'possum.

"All right." Salvador tapped his watch. "Let's head to our next location. Maybe we can catch some ghost lights."

Tall pines and cypress trees shrouded Bragg Road in a dense gloom. The Monster Busters team walked along the eerie stretch of road, feet crunching in the loose gravel.

"We're gonna turn 'round at the ghost town," Dingo told the audience, turning to walk backward for a few moments.

"We should turn around *now*." Marquis stopped.

"We aren't far from Bragg Station," Salvador coaxed.

Marquis shook his head. "I have a bad feeling about this. Real bad. Please, let's go now."

"Come on, Marquis." Dingo strode over and patted his friend on the back. "This isn't like you."

"Guys?" Julie's voice trembled.

The cameraman turned his device to the trees. A dozen pairs of eyes glowed like rogue embers in the dense forest. The Monster Busters clustered together in the center of the road.

Fortunately for the live TV audience, the creatures took the cameraman first.

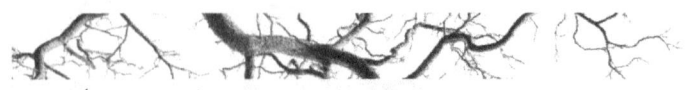

Taking Liberties with the Dead
By David Welling

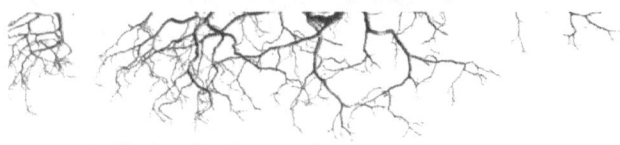

L ITTLE pig, little pig, let me in.

Not by the hair of my chinny-chin-chin.

So it remains a part of the popular mythology along with crosses, wooden stakes, and sleeping in a coffin during the daylight hours. Rule: The threshold of a home cannot be crossed unless an invitation is extended first from one already inside. So often has this been repeated in countless novels and movies that it is accepted as an unquestionable fact.

What bullshit.

Curtis rang the doorbell, then gave it another jab for good measure. After a half minute, he heard footsteps on the other side before the door opened.

Curtis grinned, fashionably late as usual. Black Nirvana T-shirt, black jeans, white tennis shoes, hair short, but not too short, and his typical *who-cares* expression on his face. A small ice cooler hung from his left hand, the size appropriate for a six-pack, with some dozen holes drilled into the top. A soft, rustling noise could be heard from within.

Facing him from the inside stood Kelsey, a stark comparison if there ever was one. Where Curtis was lanky and thin, Kelsey was the Oliver Hardy equivalent, looming over him by a few extra inches vertically, and more than a few in width. Big guy, to be sure. This expanse was covered by a Hawaiian shirt and weathered blue jeans, an attire worn more for comfort than style.

"Don't believe in getting here early, do ya?" he quipped. "It's getting ready to start."

"Good to see you too."

Curtis stepped into the short corridor as the door shut behind him. They took a left directly through the kitchen to the living room beyond. The space appeared quite clean, immaculately dusted and vacuumed with everything in its place. Kelsey was neat to a fault with his environment, a contradiction to his less-than-spotless appearance. Trina, the mistress of the house, mirrored such meticulous attention but speculation suggested she merely adopted some of his habits by association. Kelsey and Trina always played the ideal hosts.

The rest— Larry, Helen, C. J., and Stacey—had already arrived, making themselves comfortable in the living room, reclining in the chairs and sofas surrounding the television. The room itself was small with most of the space taken by the furniture.

Dark wood paneling, clearly dating the décor to an era three or four decades prior, made the room masculine and dark. The dim lighting was enhanced by the windows covered with black Foam-core board taped into place with black masking tape. As with everything else in the house, it was done with methodical precision.

The placement of these panels effectively eliminated any light from coming through, either the artificial kind from the nearby streetlights at night or the real thing during the day. Such window treatments were found on every other window in every other room of the house.

This was hardly unusual. Curtis had done the same with his dwelling—and for that matter, the rest of the guests had as well.

"Hey, guys."

The response to this greeting varied. Stacey looked with a cheerful smile along with a gaze that clung to him a second longer than usual. "Hi, Curt." With that, she directed her attention back to the television. C. J.'s response was more economical in action with a simple wave of his hand. His eyes never left the screen. On the couch, Trina, Larry, and Helen were already engrossed in the program and offered no acknowledgment.

Larry pointed to the set. "Show's starting." Curtis accepted this to be as much of a "hello" as he would get from the group at least until the first commercial break. He made his way to an unoccupied chair next to Stacey, placed his cooler to the side, and sat.

The center of attention before them was a television of the furniture variety, a large console that assuredly dated back to the Seventies. That it still worked was a wonder, and despite constant prompting to upgrade the TV, Kelsey held firm to the vintage model. The tube worked, the picture was clear, the color satisfactory, and the speakers still produced a crisp sound. Anyway, cable made a difference; not like the old days with the rabbit-ear antenna and horrible reception. Kelsey had obviously made adjustments for the old technology to work with the new.

It functioned, which was enough. And *The Vampire Maulers* was on.

Guitar wails and a frenetic drumbeat blasted through the room as the opening credits ran their course. A quick montage of scenes from previous episodes was interspersed with still shots of the show's ensemble cast beginning with the lead, a cosmetic cover girl/model-turned-actress.

Clad in black, skin-tight leather, and weapons in hand, her image was shown in a rapid succession of clips—fighting, kicking, and staking—in all, a well-displayed bit of choreography. Against this imagery were the antagonists of the show—a wide variety of vampires, werewolves, demons, mutants, poltergeists, ghosts, ghouls, gremlins, hell-hounds, psychos, incubi, succubi, zombies, witches, aliens, serpents, beasties, imps, ogres, flesh-eating fiends, mad scientists, inter-dimensional entities, lecherous leprechauns, possessed classmates, possessed postal workers, possessed toasters, fanatical moms, and even a demonic squirrel.

But that was what *Vampire Maulers* was all about—teen assassins taking out the undead, one wooden stake at a time.

Accented by a ghastly, maniacal laugh, the credits faded to a graveyard scene around midnight and their leader, Ellie, alone on patrol. A hooting owl broke the silence. A close-up framed her face on the right side of the screen with the background clearly visible over her shoulder—the standard setup for a jump scare.

The vampire materialized from behind, taking her by surprise. Instinctively, she averted his attack and struck back. As the camera panned past the tombstones, the two leaped and kicked at one another in a battle of will and strength.

With an inhuman force, the vampire knocked Ellie to the ground, then pounced on her with teeth bared. With a forceful kick, she pushed him back and rose to her feet once more. Stake in hand, she lunged forward and plunged the weapon deep into the creature's chest. He let out a horrifying cry, clutching the air about him, then exploded into a spray of fine, undead dust. Another vampire bit the big one.

Curtis shook his head at the effects. "So fake."

"As if you know," Kelsey replied.

"Okay, I've never taken a stake—but vamps do not go poof and turn into fairy dust when they're offed. When you're down, you're down, and that's the end. This is all so Hollywood."

"Personally, I like it," C. J. commented. "Makes the fight more dramatic." He reached toward the side table for the glass half filled with a thick, red liquid. He took a swig and stifled a belch.

"Just once, give me reality," Curtis replied. "It's like the script-writers are all trying to outdo each other."

"Do you mind?" said Helen, clearly annoyed at the interruption.

C. J. ignored her remark. "Who wouldn't prefer a dramatic exit? I'd much rather go out like Darth Vader than Winnie the Pooh."

Curtis raised an eyebrow. "Did the Pooh bear die?"

"Doesn't matter."

Onscreen, Ellie studied the dusty remains of her opponent, finding a gold ring in the ashes. After careful examination and noting the cryptic symbols engraved on the sides, she pocketed the jewelry and walked offscreen. Fade out.

As a set of commercials began, Curtis looked about the room. "So, where's Chet? I thought he was coming."

"Obviously he found a better offer," Kelsey remarked.

Larry broke his attention from the TV. "He doesn't dig the horror stuff. Rather watch a ball game."

"He has a point," Stacey remarked. "We could try watching something light for a change." Her comment raised a few smiles. She was hardly a *Maulers* fan either, but always showed up for the company.

Trina had been relatively quiet until now. "I think Larry shushed him one too many times."

"Hey," Larry replied, "I was watching the show. He got too loud. If he wants to yak, do so in the kitchen."

Helen snapped at the comment. "Like now? The show's back on. Can we have some quiet please?"

With that, the conversation eased in volume, and attention returned to the TV. The Mauler Squad sat at a table, engaged in resolving the ring mystery, passing the trinket from one to another. None were able to decipher the mystical symbology.

Curtis reached over to his cooler and opened the top. After a moment of fumbling, he pulled out a little ball of fur. The kitten was a mixed-breed tabby with short hair and wide eyes. The animal brought forth an immediate coo from Stacey.

"Ohhh, she's so cute. Can I hold her?" With a smile, Curtis passed the animal over. Stacey immediately fawned over the creature while stroking its back. "What an adorable little thing. And look at those big eyes. Does she have a name?"

"No. Not that it matters."

"Well, we all live for the moment, don't we, kitty?" she said to the furball, kissing it on the head. She ran her fingers softly across its back for a while longer, occasionally reaching underneath to scratch its neck. Then, with a sigh, she passed the kitten back to Curtis. "Fare thee well, little thing."

Curtis repeated the process, petting the cat absentmindedly while watching the program. At length, he affectionately picked the animal up and rubbed his cheek against it, feeling the warmth of its body and listening to the soft purr. He, too, kissed it several times, and then with a quick deftness, opened his mouth, sank his fangs deep into the creature, and drank.

Kelsey shot him a glance. "Hey! Don't spill anything on the furniture."

Curtis did not reply except for a nod. At length, he looked up to meet Stacey's gaze with the slightest smile and an expression of both empathy for the animal and desire motivated by her hunger. The tip of her tongue came into view, running across her upper lip, then back across her teeth, feeling the pointed ends.

"Care for a slurp?" he asked, raising his head to return the smile. She extended her hands for the offering, motivating Kelsey to pass a plate to her. "Here. Use this."

"I'll be neat, but thank you anyway," she replied, taking the kitten in her hands. By this time, the purring had stopped. She buried her head in the fur and drank deeply, emitting a *yummy* sound in the process. Kelsey looked from her to the plate and then set it on the table. "It's right here with the napkins if you need it," he said with a sigh.

"I could use a drink myself," said Larry, stretching his legs as the program went to yet another commercial break. "You got anything warm, Kelsey?"

"It's in the kitchen. Help yourself."

"Thanks. How about you?" he asked Helen.

"I'm all right. I'll just have a sip of whatever you're having." Larry made his way from the living room in search of something body temperature and drinkable as the rest lapsed into silence. Helen glanced at Kelsey. "So how come you talk during the show but shut up during the ads?"

"Because it pisses you off."

"Just once will you put a cork in it so I can watch the episode undisturbed? That's why we come over here every week, right?"

"It's a social thing. Yeah, there's the show, but—you know—bonding."

"Mmm," Stacey purred, who lowered the kitty from her lips. "Curt, there's not much left. I'm afraid I got carried away."

"Take the rest. I ate before I came."

A wolf's howl from the TV signaled the end of the commercials. "Show's back on," Helen called.

"Now what were we talking about?" Kelsey snickered with a passing glance at Helen.

"Oh, piss off and pipe down."

Leaning forward, Stacey placed the fuzzy carcass on the plate, running her hands over the fur several times in a gesture of affection before reaching nearby for a napkin. Her tongue made a series of passes across her lips followed by a tidy wipe of the napkin and all traces of her snack were swept away.

Larry eyed the lifeless kitten as he walked back from the kitchen. "I just can't handle the domestic animal taste." In one hand, he carried a glass partially filled with red liquid, which sloshed around as he walked, coating the upper edges with a softer pinkish-brown hue.

"So who asked you?" Curtis replied. "You don't like it, don't drink it. It's still better than that pre-packaged crap you have there."

"Maybe so, but at least it's not a fuzzy."

"I like mine warm and fresh. As to the species, it has a more complex taste and an exceptional finish. Things don't always have to be meat and potatoes, to borrow a phrase."

Kelsey laughed. "Always the snob, eh, Curtis?"

"Yes, I am. Look, everyone has different strokes. Some mortals like Mexican food and some don't. Others prefer Chinese, Mediterranean, or American. It is a matter of personal likes and an acquired taste. I wouldn't eat it all the time—I like a bit of variety in my life."

"So you're partial to Chinese?" Kelsey responded as much to Curtis as everyone else in the room.

"Yeah, depends on the mood and if one is available. But I'm an equal opportunity feeder."

Stacey looked down, then spoke in a soft voice, slightly embarrassed. "You may not believe this, but—I've never tried one."

"Really?" Trina asked with a distinct note of surprise in her voice. "I love Chinese food."

"The opportunity never has come up."

"Well, we may just have to do something about that," Curtis said with a gleam in his eye, eager to help expand her horizons.

Larry shook his head once more, bringing the conversation back to the plate before them. "I just don't do animals. It's degrading and I don't like the taste of fur. If we were meant to eat them, we'd still be warm-bloods."

"Oh!" Kelsey exclaimed. "That is so profound."

"Bite it, Kels!"

"I usually do."

Drinking from his glass, C. J. tried to stifle his laughter, nearly sending projectile blood across the table.

"Photo op," Curtis snickered. "Too bad I didn't have a camera."

"Wouldn't do you any good, anyway."

"I used to keep a scrapbook of photos," Stacey said. "Memories, experiences, things I did, places I went, people I knew, all there. No point in that now, but I miss it. Like us sitting here week after week. There is no way to record that except in my mind, my memories—and sometimes, memories fade. Especially as the years go on. It's not fair."

Kelsey felt a similar pang. "Who said things were fair?"

Curtis mused over this. "No mirrors, no cameras, no video. You would think that with all this technology, there might be a workaround."

Stacey let out a sigh, sinking farther into the couch, adding, "I would so love to see myself once more, watch while I comb my hair, put on makeup. It's been so long."

Curtis patted her on the back. "You don't need any makeup."

"You're sweet."

"Actually, I side with Curtis," C. J. said, having now wiped his mouth clean. "There's something about the fur. I like the way it tickles my nose."

Curtis interlocked his hands with the two index fingers pointing out to Larry. "You see? Tomato, tomato. Potato, potato," he said, changing the pronunciation each time. "Different strokes."

Helen, who had been growing more irritated as the conversation progressed, interrupted with a voice louder than usual. "Kelsey, do you mind if I turn up the volume?"

Kelsey walked over to the set and bumped up the sound, just barely, hardly noticeable to anyone listening. "How's that?"

Her response, as expected, was an ice-cold "Right. Thanks."

"Kelsey, if you had a newer TV, you could change the volume with a remote, and you wouldn't have to get up," Curtis noted.

"The set works fine."

"The new ones are better."

"This one's fine."

"Dude, this antique belongs in the grave. It's been around longer than you've been dead. What does that say?"

"That we belong together."

"I give up," Curtis said with a wave of his hand, accepting defeat. "It's your place. Do what you will."

"I don't even have a TV," C. J. added. "I can't complain."

"But I can," complained Helen. "Will you guys shut up?"

Kelsey figured it was time to cool the temperature. "All right, princess, just for you."

"Thank you."

All eyes returned to the television, and silence enveloped the room just as the scene faded out for another five minutes of commercials. Someone in the room—not Helen—found this to be incredibly funny.

Kelsey rose, taking advantage of the break to tidy up a bit. He scooped up the plate with the kitty carcass along with the soiled napkins and carried them to the kitchen.

Larry cast a glance at the group. "So Helen and I are going out to eat afterward. Anyone else care to join us?"

"Sounds good," said C. J. "Where to?"

"Haven't decided yet. Any thoughts?"

"Something easy tonight—fast food. I don't want to have to hunt too hard for my meal."

"Trina? Kelsey?"

Trina shook her head. "I don't feel like getting out tonight."

"How about you, Stacey?"

"Oh, I don't know," she said, looking at Curtis in a manner that indicated full well how she would prefer to spend the rest of the evening. "I haven't decided yet."

His eyes met hers with a clear understanding and a similar want. They had always fared well together, never quite full partners, but something close. The slightest knowing smile along with a nod confirmed it for her.

"—but I think I'll pass."

The final batch of commercials ran their course, leading into the end segment of *Vampire Maulers*. Onscreen, the villains of the week surrounded Ellie and her mates. A few bits of witty dialogue and a swell of the music signaled the final fight of the episode. Always well-choreographed, a ballet of kicks, thrusts, moves, and countermoves followed, all foreplay to the impalement and subsequent transformation into ashtray residue.

And Ellie never broke a sweat.

"Nice hair," Curtis noted. "Every strand is absolutely perfect."

"Another plausibility check?" C. J. asked.

"You bet. No matter how intense the battle, every week she looks perfect. Believable? I think not. At least they could muss up her hair."

Larry chuckled. "You are, after all, talking about a show that has werewolves and zombies as regulars. How real is that? You have to suspend your disbelief a bit."

"There are no such things as werewolves."

"Just like there are no such things as vampires?"

"Screw you, Larry. You know what I mean, and as far as mortals are concerned, we don't exist—except in bad movies and TV shows like this—then we're given nasty attitudes, a horrible complexion, and names like Dagger or the Count of Darkness. Why can't they have normal names like Joe or Scooter? Have them do pedestrian things like working a night shift, making minimum wage, or shopping for Solo cups at an all-night grocery store? And never, never, do you see a vampire doing something truly mundane like brushing their teeth."

"You're right about one thing—mortal perceptions," Stacey agreed. "No one believes in us except as pure fantasy. I certainly didn't believe until I transitioned, and even then—well, there's that denial stage."

Trina understood the feeling well. "We all go through that, the five stages of death: denial, resentment, bargaining, depression, and acceptance. It all changes when we drink for the first time."

"That is my point. That's real. What is so difficult in adding that to the show?"

"Probably because the writers are human," C. J. noted before taking another swig of his drink.

Kelsey stretched his arms above him, working a kink from his shoulders. "It would be nice to see an alternate point of view. Just because you're dead doesn't necessarily mean you're bad. How about a kid-friendly vampire?"

"That's not the way lifers see it. If the ticker don't tick, then you must be a creature from hell. It's all black and white, no grays. The unspoken motto of *The Maulers* is simple: the only good vampire is a dead one. End of story."

A touch of melancholy swept across Stacey's face. "It's rather sad, all this prejudice."

Curtis shook his head. "It's not prejudice. That only applies to what people accept as real. We're not real, not to the living—we are the stuff that scary stories are made from. Since we do not exist to mortals, there is no true hatred for our kind. How can you be anti-vampiric when you consider us to be mythic? It would be as silly as bigotry against elves and unicorns. Mortals don't buy in. No vampires, therefore, no prejudice."

Kelsey shook his head in mock disgust. "I hate unicorns."

"So do I," Larry mirrored.

Curtis pointed to the TV. "That's the true villain there, the media. And a series that downgrades our kind with a few special effects. We are nothing more than stereotypes of the simplest form."

"That's Hollywood for you."

The final scene drew to a close on the TV: a close-up of Ellie looking particularly pissed in a glamorous, fashionable sort of way, then a fade to black. The credits appeared, then all conversation ceased as the brief clips from next week's episode flashed across the screen, an irony that more attention was given to the few seconds of teasers than the entire show that preceded it.

With that, the show ended. Kelsey rose and turned the set off. "Can anyone tell me what happened in the show tonight? I missed some of it." Helen offered not a word, but her glare said it all.

Larry rose from the couch and rubbed his hands together. "Not one to watch and run, but I am starving. Are you ready, Helen?" She nodded and rose.

"What about you, C. J.? Joining us?" he continued.

"You bet. The night is still young and alive."

The trio said their good-byes and made their way to the door. As they stepped outside, Helen mumbled to Larry, "Damned loud mouths. Next week, you can come by yourself. I'll stay home where it's quiet."

Trina occupied herself in the kitchen, cleaning the mess left behind and washing glassware with the red liquid mixing with the water before sliding down the drain. After a quick wipe with a towel, the glasses were placed on the shelf.

Kelsey returned to his guests in the living room where conversation resumed. Neither left right away. For Stacey, common courtesy remained alive, even when someone else wasn't, and it was only proper to pace your exit. To leave immediately after the program ended would have been rude. After a while, however, Kelsey excused himself to the kitchen.

Curtis took a step toward her. "Any plans for the rest of the night?"

Stacey smiled a radiant smile. Her canines, sharp and white, were visible for a moment, then hidden behind her lips. She looked down, then back to Curtis. "No," she replied simply.

"Hungry?"

She nodded. He came closer and spoke in a voice that was both gentle and inviting. "I know a good place."

Her tongue appeared, just slightly, moistening her lips, then again, a smile. "Let me get my things."

After collecting her purse and jacket, and he his cooler, they made their way to the front door, said their good-byes, and stepped into the cool air outside.

"See you later," Kelsey said with a final wave. He closed and locked the door, then took a deep breath, feeling the silence that now permeated the house.

"They gone?" Trina's voice came from the living room.

"All gone."

"Good." She appeared around the corner, the last dirty glasses and plates in hand, and walked them to the kitchen. "Why can't we ever do this at someone else's house?"

"Tradition. Everyone likes it here."

"But we get stuck with the cleanup." She set the remaining dishes in the sink before rambling back to the living room. A moment later, her voice exploded. "Shit, your friends got blood on the sofa again."

Outside, Curtis and Stacey reached the end of the driveway and stopped.

"Which way?" she asked.

"Left. I was thinking … Chinese."

He took her hand, and she wrapped her fingers around his. Together, they sauntered along the sidewalk, then away together, allowing themselves to be comfortably enveloped by the night.

TRAPS

By A. B. Richards

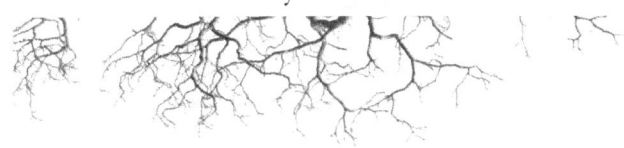

CARSON Miller slammed his truck door and spat. Late October frost crunched under his boots as he hiked out to check his traps. He was no closer to finding a job, and he really needed that coyote bounty money to keep the lights on.

He grinned as he approached the first trap. A large male coyote tried to run away from him, and screamed in pain as the short chain played out and yanked the swollen foot vised in a steel jaw trap.

"Nothin' personal, dude," Carson told the song dog before he shot it, putting it out of its misery.

If he had another way to get money right now, he would. That wasn't exactly right. His cousin had offered him work at the car wash. That was a job for a high school kid, not a grown man. Carson didn't mind taking the 'yotes. There were plenty of them. But he didn't relish it, either.

Unlike Billy Henson. Carson shuddered. The things he did to the animals he caught would make a serial killer queasy. He was the one who'd told him how trapping was easy money on the one and only time he went hunting with Billy. Never again. He'd had nightmares for weeks. Although some of the other guys didn't seem to mind. He shook his head. What could he do about it, anyway?

He only needed the coyote's ears and tail for the bounty, so he cut them off. The pelt was worth good money, so he took that, too, and left the rest for scavengers. He took the trap with him—he'd have to move it to a new location because the coyotes would avoid this place for a while.

"What the hell?"

The second trap was smashed and broken on the rocks. He saw human tracks, canine tracks. And a bent rabies tag. *Oops. Well, people shouldn't let their dogs run loose. It was their own fault.*

He huffed as he picked up the twisted metal. It was beyond repair, another item he couldn't afford to replace. Then he laughed bitterly. *Guess that's what I get for taking career advice from a psycho.*

The third trap was sprung, but there was no animal in it. Sometimes they'd chew off a paw to escape. Carson didn't know if they lived or died after that. Sad, but it happened.

As he got closer, he saw blood on the ground. Now, he'd have to move this one, too.

Carson swore. Next to the trap were three toes. Not bear. Not canid or big cat. Human. Three bloody human toes.

Should I call somebody? The sheriff? Game warden?

He poked the severed digits with a stick.

The guys know I've got traps out here. Is this a Halloween prank?

He picked one up and threw it to the ground. It was human, alright.

Shit.

While it was true that there was no season or bag limit on coyotes, he'd known when he'd set the trap yesterday that it was too close to a hiking trail. But it was a perfect spot, and how many people were out here hiking at this time of year, anyway? Especially barefooted?

At least one.

Carson ran his hands across his scalp and grabbed fistfuls of his thick, dark hair. Calling the sheriff wasn't an option, that's for sure. Putting a trap that close to a trail was only a misdemeanor, but it carried a fine. Even worse, if someone got hurt in one of his traps, they'd sue the crap out of him. They could take everything he had and still get nothing. But it was his nothing.

He scooped up the toes and shoved them into the bag with the coyote parts. He grabbed the trap and jogged back to his truck. As he approached the Mansford River bridge, he slowed to let a black SUV pass him, and when that vehicle rounded a curve, Carson pulled over. He flung the trap over the railing, then fumbled in his pouch for the toes. Gagging as he tossed them into the foaming water one by one, he waited for the dry heaves to stop before he dared to get back behind the wheel.

Gravel crunched behind him. Carson whirled to see a black and white patrol car pulling up behind his truck.

Deputy Mel Stafford got out. "Carson? You okay?"

"Uh." Carson flashed a short-lived grin at his friend. "Yeah. Yeah, I'm fine. I just, um, thought I saw someone in the water down there." He shook his head, his shoulders jerking into a shrug. "It was nothing. Just a tree limb."

"Well, that was neighborly of you to stop and check it out. You got time for a cuppa joe in town?"

"Not this morning. Got to get to the extension office." *Idiot! Why did you tell him that? Now he'll know you've been checking your traps.*

"Next time."

"Yeah. See ya 'round."

Deputy Mel pulled away as Carson started his truck. *You'd better hope no one with seven toes shows up at the sheriff's office.*

Carson collected his coyote bounty and worked on preparing the pelt. He was so distracted he almost ruined it twice. His stomach still clenched at the thought of food, so when dinnertime rolled around, he had a beer or three. The floor of his trailer creaked and groaned as he paced back and forth, avoiding the sagging spot that might not take his weight.

It was after two when he finally dropped onto his bed and exhaustion took him down. He wasn't sure what time it was when he sat bolt upright with a gasp, sure something had touched him. The skin on his right arm still tingled where only moments ago, he was certain cold, bony fingers had grabbed him.

Nothing moved in the dark, and as far as Carson could tell, everything was exactly how he had left it when he flipped off the lights. He thought he detected the faintest odor of something dead, but decided it was probably the coyote blood on his clothes. He should have thrown them in the wash before he hit the sack.

Carson pulled the ragged quilt up around his neck and stared at the ceiling. Outside, something snuffled at the window. He silently grabbed the shotgun from under his bed and peered through the grimy glass. The noise stopped, but the soot-black night hid any creature in the vicinity.

He started to open the window but thought better of it. If the animal was a coyote, the blast would wreck the pelt. If it was a bear, the season was open, but he didn't have a permit. Cost extra, and why waste freezer space on greasy bear meat when he could fill it with venison?

He sighed and returned to the warmth of his blanket.

Six o'clock seemed to come sooner than expected. He got up, and as he pulled off his tee-shirt, noticed a rash on his right arm. Right where he was sure he'd been touched last night. Whelp, that mystery was solved. He must have brushed up against some poison ivy, and it had started to kick in during the night. Carson didn't remember taking off his jacket, but clearly he did at some point. The rash wasn't itchy, though. Just red.

After a breakfast of dry toast and coffee, he set out to check his remaining trap. The wreckage of the other one was still in his truck. He'd sell it for scrap at the junkyard later.

When he arrived, the trap was closed. No blood or hide on it. Just closed. He checked the chain, and it was still firmly attached to the tree. He stepped on the side levers to open the trap, but as he was moving the pin, his foot slipped and the steel jaws snapped shut on his forearm. A shout of pain rocketed from his throat.

Carson struggled to get his feet back on the levers, but lost his balance and thudded to the ground, the implacable metal biting deeper into his arm. He whimpered and tried to stand, but each movement tugged on the trap. Carson crawled over to the tree, hoping to release the chain so he could get out of the woods and get help. But he needed both hands to turn the nut on the end of the bolt that held the links together. He felt nothing below the searing, throbbing pain where the trap's jaws held his arm.

He spent hours trying every trick he knew, but nothing worked. He was hungry. He was thirsty. The pain in his arm seemed to have a mind of its own, surging and retreating; burning, then stabbing. Working its way up his arm and into his chest, up his neck into his head, the pain was a boa constrictor, wrapping him in its unwelcome embrace and slowly suffocating him.

Every struggle amplified his suffering, so after a while, Carson just lay still, panting. It was then he noticed that the trap had closed exactly on the streak of poison ivy. He tried to pass it off as a weird coincidence. But the bitter, metallic taste of fear oozed through his parched mouth.

Maybe a hiker or another trapper will come by. Or maybe I'll just lay here and die. Not sure which is better at this point.

As the sun closed in on the horizon, he pulled his buck knife out of its leather holster. Carson suspected the bones in his arm were broken, and it was completely numb below the trap. If he didn't want to be bear bait, he was going to have to do something drastic. People survived amputations every day. They did not often survive hungry bears, who would be eager to pack on that last bit of winter fat as they denned up to hibernate. Especially pregnant females.

There was a full clip in his .22, but even if he did hit it shooting left-handed, it would just make a large bear mad. People went missing around here, especially hunters, and Carson had always figured they'd either fallen down a rocky crevasse or got the short end of a dispute with a bear or cougar.

Gripping the handle of the knife, he clenched his teeth.

The bushes near him rustled. Carson turned his head, trying to minimize any movement to his arm. The canid that approached him looked like a coyote but was the size of a timber wolf. It limped and Carson was stunned to see that it was missing three toes from its left hind foot. The wounds were fresh.

He waved the knife. "Get out of here! Get!"

Carson would have to roll over to reach his gun and he deeply and sincerely hoped it didn't come to that.

The animal circled him, then stopped in line with Carson's face, about five feet away. The dog shimmered and rippled, and then a man stood there.

At least, he thought it was a man. The entity in front of him had black and white paint on his entire body. Tangled black hair bushed out from under the pelt-covered skull of a coyote that perched atop his head. The dog's lower jaw was fastened on so it seemed the man's face peered out from the throat of a coyote. And as far as Carson could tell, that was the extent of his wardrobe.

The man sniffed the air like an animal and chuckled.

"Stay away from me! I'm armed!" Carson's voice broke. He had little fight left in him.

The man laughed. "If I wanted you dead, I would have killed you last night." His voice was deep and gravelly.

Two more men, similarly dressed, joined the first. One of them coughed. "Told you he'd be here."

Carson stared at the toe stumps in front of him, and the bloody nubs made his stomach churn. He figured his best plan was to be still, until they released him, then he'd sprint away. They wouldn't be expecting that. Hopefully.

The original interloper reached behind his back and retrieved a pouch that had been hidden underneath the pelt. The other two men began chanting, and the man with the pouch opened it and sprinkled white powder all over Carson's body.

"What are you doing?" he demanded, but the three ignored him. He hoped it wasn't meat tenderizer.

The pouch man joined the others in the last round of chanting, and they finished with a single shouted word. Then they howled like a pack of coyotes. There was an answer in the distance, and Carson hoped it was actual canines. The thought of another group like this roaming the forest chilled him more than the October air. The two chanting men each stepped on a lever of the trap, opening the jaws. Carson yanked his arm free and rolled away from the men.

He bounded down the trail, the adrenaline that flooded his body knocking out most of the pain in his arm. Carson was more than halfway back to his truck when he realized he was on all fours. That fact shocked him enough to stop him in his tracks.

He looked down at his hands, only to see beige paws. Coyote paws. He sat down hard on his rump.

What the actual—

A smell on the wind flashed a red alert in his brain. Salty. Sour. Men. Men were coming this way and he needed to be gone. Like yesterday. He loped in the opposite direction. The adrenaline was ebbing and pain flowed in to take its place. Carson slowed to a limping walk.

This is some crazy dream. Or I'm hallucinating from the pain. Wait, what did that guy put on me? Angel dust or something? Acid? Gotta get back to my house. I'll be safe there. And when this shit wears off…

He stood on the crest of a wooded ridge. Down below, he saw a glowing red sign—a medical cross and the word 'EMERGENCY.'

Yes. They'll take care of me there. They'll fix my arm and might have an antidote to whatever this drug is.

As the crow flies, or the coyote trots, Carson reckoned the hospital was about half a mile away, possibly a little more. He picked his way along the stony path as fast as he was able. He felt nothing but relief as the automatic door slid open.

The woman at the intake desk jumped to her feet and screamed. The handful of people in the waiting area gasped and shouted. Deputy Mel, who worked a second job as a security guard, ran down the corridor toward Carson, his hand on his holstered gun.

"Mel! I need help!" Carson tried to say, but the sound that came out of his jaws was *yip, yip, yip*. He turned and fled back to the forest.

It took the rest of the night, but he made his way back to his house. He had neither keys nor opposable thumbs, so he used his snout to push a broken piece of lattice out of the way and crawled under the trailer.

Two weeks had passed, and Carson had lost weight. He felt the skin and fur glide over his rough ribs with each breath. His front leg was still sore, but the pain was manageable now. He was terrible at hunting the few mice that hadn't hidden away in their burrows for the winter. Mostly, he traveled to the edge of town and raided garbage cans.

One night, a fat raccoon waddled up to share a meal. He tried to convert it to dinner, but the furry fury clamped its sharp teeth over his nose and clawed at his eyes, chittering angrily the whole time. A door opened, and the raccoon let go. Carson fled.

As he galloped along the path under the trees, something grabbed his good front leg and he crashed to the ground, yelping.

Shit. Shit. Shit. Shit.

He knew who set traps in this area. Billy Henson—a fate worse than death—lived just around the bend. A three-legged coyote may not be a good hunter, but dumpsters didn't move very fast. Hell, even starving to death was a better prospect than falling into Billy's sadistic hands.

Carson started to gnaw at the fur of his leg just above the jaws of the trap.

A twig snapped behind him. Carson pinned his ears and snarled as the over-sized coyote padded up to him. He'd only seen coyotes this size once before, and his stomach dropped. It started a yipping howl while Carson growled in fear. *Is he calling the rest of the pack to tear me to pieces?*

The hind foot. Three toes missing. The ringleader. This might be even worse. Or perhaps he was calling his cohorts to reverse the spell. He allowed a tiny spark of hope to flare in his heart.

The other two soon arrived. They also wore the shapes of wolf-sized coyotes. The three then shifted into human form and conferred softly in a language Carson didn't understand.

The man who arrived first cleared his throat. "For one year, if you survive, you are a coyote. But you can shorten the time."

Carson cocked his head, gritting his teeth against the pain in his front leg.

"If you agree to help us, I will remove the curse. We will release you from the trap and tell you of our plans. If not…" he shrugged. "You know who this trap belongs to."

I feel like whatever their plan is, it's going to be bad. But then again, it can't be worse than Billy.

He nodded carefully, keeping his trapped leg as still as possible.

As before, the two men stepped on the side levers, and Carson jerked his foot away from the hateful steel. As the man talked, he sat and licked the bloody wound he'd chewed on his leg.

"We guard this forest as best we can. Those who do not respect the land feed it with their blood. There is one we have been seeking for some time." The man's eyes fell on the empty trap and his lips pressed into a scowl. "He has caused great harm—his very bloodline is a curse. Tonight, you will help put an end to it."

Carson nodded. He wasn't any more successful as a coyote than he had been as a man. *But at least as a man I can speak. And drink beer. Beer does not get enough credit in the world.*

"He will be here soon. Put your paw next to the trap and pretend to be caught. When he comes near, make as much noise as you can to cover the sound of our approach."

Carson had begun to drowse off when footsteps shuffling through the forest litter caught his attention. He pricked his ears and sniffed the air. Sour and greasy. Billy. As soon as his safety orange cap came into view, Carson started making the biggest racket he was able. Snapping, snarling, yipping, howling, any noise he could force out of his muzzle.

Billy laughed as he got closer.

That's it. Keep coming.

"Let's have some fun, doggie." Billy's lips parted in a rotten grin.

Alright guys. Where are you? Billy was getting too close for comfort.

He leaned over Carson, pulling out a small blade from his belt. Carson leaped forward and bit him on the cheek with everything he had.

Billy screamed and dropped the knife, covering his face with his hands. Three furry shapes lunged out of the trees and fell upon him.

Carson spat blood out of his mouth and wiped his lips. His human lips. He got to his feet and checked his jeans pockets. His keys were still there. Trying to ignore the wet crunching and tearing sounds, Carson made a wide berth around the heaving furry masses of the giant coyotes and what was left of Billy.

It was no small thing to kill a man, but Billy's exit left the world a better place. That was one of the few things Carson was sure of.

It was a bit of a hike back to his truck, but the air was cold and fresh. *Wonder if that car wash job is still open?*

FINDING SHIRLEY

By A. B. Richards

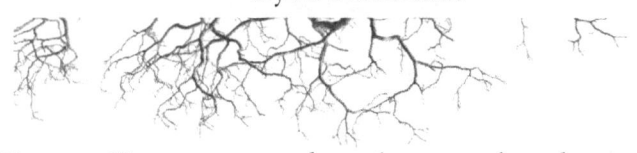

NATALIE Freemont gaped at the news broadcast she was watching on her phone. A tearful couple stood with the local police chief, explaining to news cameras that their six-year-old daughter, Shirley, had disappeared last night at the Halloween trunk-or-treat at their church.

The reporter pushed the mic toward the father. "She was wearing a blue princess dress and white plastic go-go boots. Her favorite. Hardly ever takes them off. Please, please bring my baby back."

Natalie's eyes were suddenly wet. Missing children were always a punch to the gut. The bells on the door jangled, and she hastily blotted her tears away to go to the front of the store and greet her ten o'clock.

"Good morning, Marigold. How are you?"

The middle-aged woman sniffed. "That's what I'm here to find out."

Natalie applied a practiced smile. "Alright, then. Let's see what the cards say. Follow me."

She led her client to a small room upstairs, hardly more than an alcove, with a heavy velvet curtain. The second floor contained four such rooms, plus an office and a storage area.

After Marigold shuffled and cut the cards, Natalie pulled the first one. A skeleton with a scythe rode a skeletal horse. A king and a beggar both lay in his wake. Death. Marigold gasped and covered her mouth with her hands.

"Don't worry." Natalie shook her head. "This card isn't about a physical death. Well, not usually. It signifies the end of a cycle. It means big changes are coming. But in this position, it's an obstacle. It's what crosses you. If you've got big changes happening, try not to let them get you too off balance. Just be prepared. You'll be fine."

Natalie laid out the rest of the cards and explained them. The Knight of Pentacles promised money was on the way, and the last card in the Celtic Cross was the Ace of Cups—new relationships. Satisfied with her future prospects, Marigold shopped for crystals and essential oil blends before she left.

The psychic had one more scheduled Tarot reading appointment, and then a walk-in came in right before close.

Both of those readings also started with the Death card.

As the assistant manager, Natalie usually opened and locked up. After the store closed and the other two employees left, she got her pendulum out. She rummaged through the drawer of maps to find one of Austin, Texas, a two-hour drive away. It was not at all unusual for clients to ask her to locate people or things, and she found them more often than she didn't. She usually started with the pendulum, then asked her guides to show her pictures, and finally drove around in her car, attempting to locate a spot that matched the mental images she'd seen.

She'd found an elderly woman with dementia just last month, but she asked the family to keep her name out of the papers. She didn't want to deal with the rabid skeptics and self-important debunkers that kind of media attention would bring, sure as flies to honey.

There was one detective in the Houston Police Department, Oliver Tisdale, who consulted her on the QT. He cleared more of his cases than most of his colleagues and tipped very well. Natalie wondered if she should give him a call to see if he knew anyone in Austin who might be receptive to her psychic assistance.

It would have to wait until tomorrow. Natalie gathered her tools into a silk bag and went into the bathroom to change into her costume for telling fortunes at a Halloween party tonight.

Dry leaves crunched under Natalie's feet as she ran. Her breath came in ragged gasps. The terrain trended uphill, and she slowed to a walk as it got steeper. She gave up and stopped to catch her breath, leaning against a blackened tree trunk. A creek babbled nearby. Bushy green pine and bare oak trees, hardly more than saplings, stretched for the sky in a broken forest of burned stumps and snags. Scrubby Texas cedars grew sporadically, and shrubs were puffy skirts that hid the spindly legs of many young trees.

Aching despair washed over her. Something bad had happened. So bad she couldn't comprehend it. The pain forced its way out through racking sobs. Then there was a loud bang, and everything went black.

Natalie woke from her dream with a start. She'd been thinking about finding Shirley when she fell asleep. *Is that what happened to her?*

She closed her eyes, trying to recall details of the vivid dream. When she thought she'd collected the pieces before they dissolved into mist, she reached for her phone and recorded a message describing the area. Satisfied she'd captured the details, she put the phone away and tried going back to sleep. Four-thirty was far too early to start her day.

By five-fifteen, she gave up and rolled out of bed. Sam, her petite black cat, stretched and fell back asleep.

Natalie put on the coffee and woke her laptop. She sipped the hot brew while she scoured the internet for places near Austin with recent, but not too recent, fires that matched the regenerating forest of her dream.

Of course. Bastrop. Terrible wildfires there about ten years ago. She got out her map and pendulum.

The amethyst pyramid glinted as it swung over the paper.

Wishing she'd been able to get off work earlier, Natalie pulled to a stop at the entry control hut and rolled down her window.

The park ranger opened the door and leaned over to look into her car. "Afternoon, ma'am. You have a reservation?"

"No. I just wanted to do a little hiking."

He nodded. "Make sure you have plenty of water. There's a camp store at the visitor center if you need some. That'll be $5, please."

She handed him a twenty, and he stepped inside to get change and print her day pass. He returned a few minutes later, handing her a piece of paper with tape on it. "Put this in your front window. Park closes for day use at 10." He wiped his forehead with a cloth. "Can't believe it's still this hot at the end of October."

"Yeah. It's been bad this year."

The ranger gave Natalie three fives and a park map. "Anything above this red line is off limits, but you can hike the other marked trails to your heart's content."

"Thank you."

The campgrounds around the small lake were congested with people. Someone would have found Shirley by now if she was in this area.

Natalie turned left. The cabins and picnic areas near the big lake were also jam-packed with campers. She kept driving. The further she got from the water, the less populated the park became. To her left, a gate to a trailhead was mostly covered by a big sign.

DO NOT ENTER

Closed for forest restoration project until further notice.
PUBLIC ACCESS PROHIBITED

Where else *would you hide a body?* Natalie searched for parking. The closest lot was a short hike away.

A few cars and cyclists passed her as she made her way to the restricted area. She paused and pretended to tie her shoe as a family of five ever-so-slowly biked past her. When she thought she was alone, she climbed over the orange plastic net fence and hurried into the trees.

The shadows stretched across the fading path. She probably had an hour and a half, two hours tops, before the sun sank behind the horizon. Natalie did not want to get caught out in the woods after dark. People rarely got attacked by coyotes, but it happened. Cougars were the more worrying predator out here in the Hill Country. Even deer could be dangerous, especially this time of year when they were in rut and the bucks were particularly aggressive.

She walked over a ridge and sat down so as not to be seen by anyone on the road. She retrieved her park map and pendulum.

After breathing deeply and centering herself, she asked aloud, "Where is Shirley? Please help me find Shirley."

The amethyst began to swing, indicating she should go further into the forbidden zone. Natalie used her cell phone to snap a picture of the landmarks and her GPS location. She would do this periodically to help find her way back. She'd been lost in a national park for nearly 48 hours once, and she had no desire to repeat the experience. The psychic put away her map and got to her feet, dusting dried grass off her butt.

A twig snapped to her left.

She whirled to see what it was. Something darted into the undergrowth. *Cougars don't come in black, do they?* But whatever it was seemed larger. She told herself that the sudden fright made it seem bigger than it really was. Apart from the rare migrant traipsing through, there were no bears in the Hill Country. At least, that's what she'd been told.

Don't run. It will chase you if you run. Turning her head to keep an eye on the trees, Natalie veered to the right. Leaves rustled as something walked a parallel path to hers, but she couldn't see more than a shadowy figure.

Natalie stopped.

The footfalls in the trees stopped.

She walked on quickly.

The steps matched her pace.

The psychic paused again to figure out what to do.

The stand of trees to her left ended about a hundred yards ahead. If they both kept going, she would find herself face to face with what was stalking her in just a few minutes.

Her heart pounded in her chest and her mouth went dry. *I can't stand here all night. I'm going to have to call the ranger station and get help.*

Natalie's hands were so sweaty the fingerprint reader did not recognize her. Her PIN, which she usually typed without thinking, evaporated from her brain.

The thing in the woods began walking again. It was moving to intercept her. Maybe she had enough lead distance to run in the other direction.

Motion caught her eye. To her left and a little behind her, stood a man in a park ranger uniform, waving at her.

The relief that coursed over her made her knees so weak they almost buckled. She hurried toward him, and he turned and walked deeper into the forest.

He must have a vehicle over there. I would have seen him if he came in through the gate. Natalie walked as fast as she could without breaking into a jog, but she couldn't get any closer to the ranger. She looked over her shoulder but didn't see any sign of the padfoot in the trees. Grunting in frustration, she tried to step up the pace. *Why won't he wait for me?*

The ranger turned right, and Natalie lost sight of him in the thicket. She picked her way through the trees and scrub as fast as she could. Decaying corpses of burned trees littered the ground and made it tough going. A low growl from an unseen animal made Natalie jerk to a halt.

Suddenly, it was in front of her. An enormous, impossible black panther. The cat fixed her with yellow eyes and flicked its tail. Natalie's breathing was so quick and shallow she got light-headed.

The beast crouched.

"N-n-nice kitty. Easy. Pspspsps." Her words were ragged scraps of speech.

Flicking an ear, the cat rose and trotted into the brush.

The sound of a vehicle made Natalie turn.

A four-wheeler approached rapidly along the barely-there trail. It appeared to be an official vehicle, with park services decals on it. *It's about time he came back.*

The ATV pulled to a stop and a man got out. "Game warden. Step out of the trees."

"Did you see that?"

"See what?"

"That black panther! Or maybe it was a melanistic cougar. Or a jaguar. I don't know, but it was huge."

"Cougars don't have a melanistic phase and there haven't' been jaguars in this part of Texas in a hundred years. Please walk toward me, hands where I can see them."

Natalie threw her hands up. "You had to have seen it!"

"I didn't see any giant black cats, ma'am." He shrugged, hand hovering near the gun at his belt. Natalie furrowed her brow. This wasn't the park ranger she'd seen earlier. He must have radioed the warden.

She raised her hands to shoulder height and started toward him. "Yes, sir. I had a… it's hard to explain." She grabbed a trunk for balance as the brittle bark she'd stepped on collapsed. "I'm looking for that missing little girl. For Shirley."

"Why do you think she'd be here?"

"Well, I'm a psychic med—"

He snorted with laughter. "Of course you are. I'm going to cite you for being in a restricted area and escort you out of the park."

"I'm sorry. I just had a fee—" Natalie tripped and crashed to the ground. She found herself face to face with a human skull.

She screamed and scrambled away.

The warden ran over and examined her find. He shook his head. "Well, I'll be damned. Looks like you *have* found Shirley."

Detective Tisdale set his coffee on the Formica diner table, grinning as he took a seat. "Only you, Nat. Only you."

A server brought their desserts and the ticket.

"I don't know who that was, but it was definitely not a six-year-old girl."

"Nope. She's been found by the way. Seems her flakey aunt decided, at the Halloween thing, to take Shirley to visit her grandparents for the weekend. Didn't think to mention it to the girl's parents. When the grands saw on TV she was missing, they called her mom and the local police."

"That's great news." Natalie tasted her coffee and stirred in more sugar.

"Yeah. You didn't fail. You just found the wrong Shirley. Jacob Shirley. He was a park ranger that went missing a month ago."

"Really? So, what do you think happened to him?"

"Well, Jake was having a fling with one of his co-workers, Tiffany. She was married and apparently started having second thoughts. When she tried to break off the relationship, Jake lost it. Evidence indicates he shot her, then disappeared. However, it was tough to untangle, given the avalanche of inaccurate tips. A witness swore they saw him in a black SUV, looking scared. Another claimed he was at the truck stop with some sketchy dudes. Still another one heard he was headed to Mexico. At the time, investigators thought that somebody, maybe a smuggler or some narcos, killed Tiffany and took Jake with them. As a hostage?" He shrugged and drank his coffee.

"Seems like it would have been the other way around—they would have taken her and, well, left him. She probably would have been easier to manage."

"Jacob Shirley had a sterling record. Everybody liked him. He went above and beyond at work. Nobody who knew him could have guessed he would do what he did. Never even occurred to his supervisor. They were sure it was foul play. Apparently, he came back to the park, overcome by his emotions at what he'd done, and ate a bullet."

Natalie broke off a piece of crust from her lemon tart. "Or somebody wanted it to look that way. You did say Tiffany was married."

"Yeah. They looked into that. Her husband was working on an offshore platform. Halfway through a two-week shift when Tiffany was killed. Between insects and scavengers, a body laying outside in the heat can skeletonize in a week. Makes time of death tough to determine, but the gun found with him was the same one that killed Tiffany, and only his prints were on it. Not saying it's impossible that somebody else killed both of them, but there's no evidence to support that."

Natalie chewed another bite of lemon tart. She hadn't found Jacob Shirley. He'd found her. But Tisdale didn't have to know that.

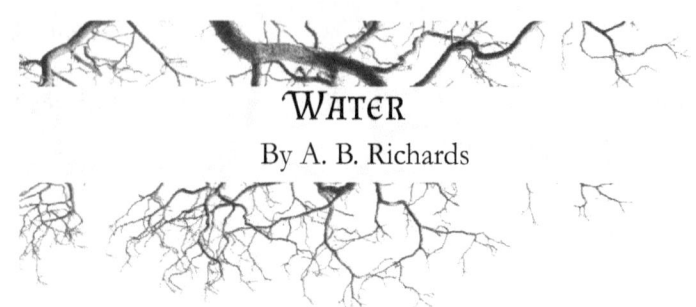

WATER

By A. B. Richards

I OPENED the front door. The stiff wind drove the torrent of rain almost horizontally, wetting the edge of my covered porch. "I'm sorry, Brandon. No trick-or-treat this year."

"It isn't fair!" He scowled at the deluge.

"I know you worked really hard on your costume. Don't forget you won first place at the zoo costume contest and got to wear it to Toby's party yesterday. So, you did get to show it off some. I understand being disappointed, though."

He sniffled. "Maybe it'll stop raining soon."

"Maybe. But the weather lady doesn't think so. And the street's flooded. See? The water's up over the sidewalk. I just don't think it's happening, Bud."

He stepped out onto the porch, as if he didn't believe me. A blaze of lightning lit up the torrent, followed by a peal of thunder that shook the house. I dodged out of the way so Brandon and his ten wiggling appendages could fit through the door as he fled back into the dry safety of the foyer, his superhero cape twisting behind him in the breeze.

He and my brother Greg—his favorite uncle—had spent hours heating and bending PVC pipes, then covering them with pool noodles to create squid arms for his Captain Kraken character. They'd made lines and dots with glow-in-the-dark paint on the arms and body, then attached flashing LEDs to the papier mâché head piece.

Greg had really stepped up since Nix disappeared a year ago. Brandon and his father were so close. I still find it hard to believe my husband would run out on his son, but… he went to the grocery store and never came back. It had rained that day, too.

I hate to think something terrible happened to him. That's horrible. But it's less horrible than the idea that he just upped sticks and abandoned his family. The man I thought I knew would never do that, not if he had a choice. It's like the Earth just opened up and swallowed every trace of Nix.

The cops think he's a runner, and I can't prove he isn't. The detective assigned to the case stopped taking my calls a couple of months ago.

I closed the door and turned to my son. "Why don't we watch a movie, huh? I'll make some popcorn while you take off your tentacles."

Brandon sighed. Loudly. "Squids only have two tentacles, Mom. The rest are arms. They have suckers all the way up. Tentacles have 'em just on the ends. The suckers have hooks inside!" He crooked his index fingers to demonstrate. "Isn't that cool?"

This is what I get for letting my brother take him to the zoo—a lecture from an eight-year-old marine biologist. Most kids want to go to Disney World. Brandon wants to go to the Monterey Bay Aquarium.

"Well, whatever they are, there isn't room on the couch for all of us."

"O. K." Brandon plodded to his room.

I went to the kitchen and measured popcorn into the microwave popcorn maker. The bursting kernels were beating against the silicone container with muffled thumps when the TV came on. I already knew which movie he'd pick. Wouldn't be long before Jack Skellington was shouting about being the Pumpkin King.

The popping slowed, nearly petering out. I turned off the microwave and divided the corn into two bowls, then sprinkled it with popcorn salt and powdered cheese. Tucking a few paper towels under my arm, I headed to the living room with the snacks.

I set the bowls on the table and settled on the sofa.

Knock. Knock! Knock!

Brandon frowned at me. "I thought you said there's no trick-or-treat."

"Maybe they have a boat."

I got up, opening the doorbell camera app on my phone as I went to see who could possibly be at my door in this weather.

The camera showed an empty porch.

Nobody's playing Ding Dong Ditch in this weather.

"Hello?" I called.

Unsurprisingly, there was no reply.

I opened the door as wide as the chain would allow and peeked through the crack. "Hello?"

No one answered. I did, however, notice that the water had risen into the yard. I wasn't *too* worried. The lot was several feet above grade, and its pier and beam construction elevated the house a yard off the ground. Still, I'd keep my eye on it.

"Who was it?"

"Nobody." I sat back down. "Must have been the wind blowing something against the door." I'd look at the doorbell footage later.

A heap of candy wrappers huddled on the table between the empty popcorn bowls. Sandy Claws had been kidnapped, and now Jack Skellington was preparing to deliver a sleighful of terrifying presents.

Thunder rattled the windows, and the power went out.

"Mom?"

"It's okay, Brandon."

I looked out the front door. Every house on the block was dark. So were the streetlights. I used my phone flashlight to locate the battery-powered camp lanterns in the front closet. *How many did I need? Two? All of them?*

The more the merrier, I decided, and grabbed all four. After bumping the door closed with my hip, I shuffled toward the coffee table.

Bang! Bang! Bang!

There was the front door again. I swallowed hard before setting the lamps down and turning one on. "There you go, Brandon."

I tapped my phone and peeked at the doorbell footage. Again, nobody was visible in the green-tinted night vision frame.

"Just the wind at the door. Let's keep it outside, okay?"

One thing I could see, though, was that the water now covered the bottom step to the front porch.

Brandon clutched the crocheted afghan around his shoulders, his eyes saucer-wide with fear. I ran my hand over his head, stopping to squeeze his shoulder.

"I have an idea." I cocked my head and gave him a grin I didn't really feel. "Why don't we build a pillow fort and play a game until the power comes back on?"

His eyes narrowed. "What game?"

I shrugged. "Uno? Trouble? Candyland?"

"Candyland is for babies. Chutes and Ladders."

We pulled off the couch cushions and draped them with blankets. Even had a mini pillow fight with throw pillows. Brandon took a lantern into the soft structure while I searched the games cabinet for the requested diversion.

The knocking started again. But this time it came from the floorboards. Something was underneath the house.

Brandon shrieked and scrambled out of the fort.

"It's okay! It's okay. Just something floating in the water. I bet it's… a tree limb. Nothing to worry about." I don't know how a tree limb could have gotten under the house, but it was the most innocuous thing I could think of at a moment's notice.

He crossed his arms and glowered. "How do you know?"

The noise stopped. I hoped it stayed quiet.

It was well past his bedtime, and I knew he was just going to get rattier as time went on. He was not going to sleep alone in his bed with this crazy storm and this off-and-on banging going on.

"Hey, Bud. Why don't you go brush your teeth and grab a book? You can sleep in my bed tonight, okay?"

Brandon nodded, and clutching a lantern in each fist, trotted off to his room. I lifted the first blanket off the fort so I could start tidying it up.

A shrill scream from the back of the house stopped my heart.

"Brandon?" I yelled, sprinting to his room.

Light shone under the bathroom door, so I flung it open. Brandon was sitting on the closed lid of the toilet, lurching from side to side as if being jolted from underneath.

"Mom!" He leapt off his perch and ran to me.

The toilet lid burst open, and a thick, suckered arm flailed in the air. Its skin was a sickly olive drab, moist and glistening. I gagged at the foul reek of rotting fish.

I froze, my brain deadlocked, trying to process the impossible information my senses fed it. In the dimmest light from the lantern, an object squirmed in the bathtub, near the drain. My first thought was that a rat or frog had come up the drain to escape the rising water. Something brushed against my arm. Like a cold, slimy tongue flicking over my flesh. Time slowed as I turned my head to see what it could be.

A smaller appendage, otherwise identical to the one in the toilet, waved from the drain in the sink.

A scream failed me as I clutched Brandon and backed out of the narrow bathroom at top speed. I tripped over the rug in the hallway and sprawled on the floor. The wood was wet. *Was water seeping up from the flood? Would that allow this thing to get into the house?*

Nausea washed over me as I struggled to my feet, slamming the bathroom door and grabbing Brandon.

Where would we go?

What room had the least plumbing?

Living room.

As I trotted over the soggy rug, I begged every god in the universe for the rain to stop. For the water to drain away. For whatever was under the house to go with it.

I set Brandon on the couch. "I'll be right back."

The lantern in the bathroom was a lost cause. No way I was going back in there. We still had three. I retrieved the one he'd left in his room. The rain and wind had let up. The house was eerily silent as I hurried back to my child.

He was not on the couch.

I gasped and whipped my head around, desperately searching. Breeze ruffled my hair.

Brandon stood in the foyer, front door wide open.

"No!" I croaked, and rushed to his side. *Who was he talking to?*

Nix stood on the front porch. My emotions ping-ponged between joy at his return and fury at his disappearance.

I put a hand on Brandon's shoulder. "Where have you been?"

"I'm sorry. It couldn't be helped." His full lips curled into a rakish grin.

"Mom! What are you doing? Let Dad in. He's back now."

I opened my mouth to tell Brandon to go fetch a towel so his father didn't drip all over the floor when he came in. But I stopped. There wasn't a droplet of water to be seen on Nix. His shoes. His pants. His fitted shirt. All dry as the Sahara. My skin prickled as the hair on the back of my neck stood up.

Nix smiled at Brandon. "I've come for my son."

"You've *what?* You think you can disappear for a year, then waltz through my front door to take my child? Oh, hell no."

"I do care for you. Maybe not in a way you can understand. I didn't want things to happen this way, but circumstances were beyond my control."

"Get out."

"Mom, no!" Brandon lurched forward and threw his arms around his father's waist.

"You're not taking him!" I growled as I leaned over and grabbed one of Brandon's arms to pry it off Nix.

My son's arm rippled in my hand. Dumbstruck, I gaped as the bone in his arm seemed to dissolve and the slimy olive drab flesh squirmed and throbbed under my fingers. It twisted and three rows of suckers gripped my forearm. I cried out as sharp barbs bit into my flesh.

Brandon's eyes were wide, and his mouth had dropped open. "Cool!" Then he let go. "Sorry, Mom! Sorry. I didn't mean it."

I stared as blood oozed from the wounds in my arm.

"Now do you believe he belongs with me?"

"I... I..."

"I never meant to hurt you. We have to go now. But I promise I'll bring him back on this day every year, so he doesn't forget his beautiful mother."

The words stuck in my throat as they stepped off the front porch into the black storm water and disappeared beneath it. The power came back on. I stared dumbly at the halo that surrounded the streetlight in the drizzle. Thunder from the retreating storm rumbled in the distance.

I stepped back and closed the door. "What a crazy dream this is! I wish I'd hurry and wake up."

When I woke the next morning, the flood water was gone. So was Brandon. I ran from room to room calling him, but deep down, I knew he wouldn't answer.

I wasn't sure what to do. No one would believe my story of what really happened, so I decided to tell anyone who asked that Brandon went to live with his dad. It wasn't untrue.

The problem is, in my shock and stupor, and my vain hope that Brandon would magically reappear the same way he'd left, I didn't think to unenroll him from school.

I'd taken four sick days from work after Nix showed up and ripped my heart out. I struggled to get out of bed to get to my job on Monday.

There was a knock at the door.

My heart leaped into my throat. I grabbed my bathrobe and ran to answer it, hope surging in my heart.

Two truant officers stood on my porch.

One of them smiled perfunctorily. "Yes ma'am. Are you Brandon Phelps' mother?"

"I am."

"Brandon has missed four days of school last week and didn't show up this morning. You haven't contacted the school. Is there a reason he's been absent?"

I blinked at them a few times. "Yes. I… I should have come down and withdrawn him. He's gone to be with his father."

"And where is that, ma'am?"

Excellent question. Wish I knew the answer. "New York." *It was as good a guess as any. But where was my baby, really?* Tears stung my eyes.

"Then you need to come down to the office and take care of the paperwork."

"Thank you. I will."

I closed the door before they could say anything else. I didn't want to fall apart in front of them.

Fortunately, Brandon's school was close enough to my office that I could handle it during my lunch hour. It was all I could do to hold in my sobs until I got to the car. I didn't want to go back to work, but I had no choice.

Later that evening, I sat on my couch staring at the TV. Don't even know what show was on. I just needed noise in the background to drown out my memories. If it was too quiet, the events of Halloween night replayed on an endless loop in my head.

Would Nix be true to his word? Would he bring Brandon to see me on Halloween? It was all I had to hold onto.

I moved one of the empty popcorn bowls over to set the remote down on the coffee table. *Had I eaten since then?* I couldn't remember.

Someone knocked on the door. I ignored it. Whoever it was would surely go away if they thought nobody was home. The clunk of brass-on-brass came again, more urgent this time.

"Brandon…?"

I hurried to the foyer, opening my doorbell app as I went.

The detective who'd stopped responding to my calls about my missing husband stood there, along with a cheerless woman I assumed was his partner.

Why are they here? Not many things I could think of that I'd rather do less than talk to these two. I opened the door. "Can I help you?"

"Yes, ma'am." His smile was grim. "May we come in? We'd like to talk to you about your missing son. You said he went to be with his father. The one you were so sure was murdered?"

Peace

By A. B. Richards

I HUGGED Lauren and Javier goodbye, sad to see them moving out. They'd been such great neighbors, and it was always a crap shoot when somebody new moved in. But that is the way of apartments. I've had quite a few neighbors over the years.

"Dixie, you're coming to the housewarming party, right?" Lauren touched my shoulder.

"Wouldn't miss it."

I wouldn't deny I was a little jealous. They'd just bought a new house with a big yard for the baby on the way and the dogs they were planning to adopt as soon as they were settled. I would kill for a big back yard.

The complex management spent a few days getting the apartment ready for new renters. I worked from home, and the industrial equipment and loud radio of the workmen passed through the walls like water through a sieve, disturbing my peace for three days. I had to decamp to a nearby coffee shop with my laptop for any hope of getting work done.

The fresh paint was barely dry when I heard the deadbolt turn next door and the thuds of something heavy being plopped on the floor. Muffled voices.

Nine PM on a Thursday seemed an odd time to be moving in, but whatever. I was busy decorating my apartment for the Halloween party I was having on Saturday. It was going to be low-key, a dozen people, if everyone and their plus one showed up. Costumes optional. Dinner. Games. Alcohol. Maybe a scary movie. I smiled at my reflection as I stuck a bloody handprint decal on the bathroom mirror.

When I was satisfied with the apartment's new look, I brushed my teeth and slipped into bed, visions of jack-o-lanterns dancing in my head.

Boom! Boom!

Thudding against the wall jolted me awake. A man shouted a string of curse words, and the wall shook again. A woman sobbed.

I pounded on my side of the wall. "Knock it off!" I shouted.

A door slammed, and the woman cried even louder.

This is not going to work out. I put my earbuds in to listen to a meditation app on my phone so I could have some peace and get back to sleep.

On Friday evening, I was struggling down the hall with too many groceries. I had overloaded myself, trying to bring everything in on one trip.

I didn't hear the footsteps until the man was too close. The greasy-haired dude in a denim vest loomed over me. Not sure if he was a biker or a biker wannabe. He looked as tough and stringy as a cheap cut of meat.

"Hey." It was more of a grunt than a word. "Lemme help you."

He snatched one of the shopping bags, dragging it painfully down my forearm.

I bent my elbow, trying to keep it from him. "I don't need your help."

He yanked the bag off my arm. "Just moved in yesterday. Tryin' to be neighborly."

Tryin' to see where I live, more likely. And if I'm home alone. But I knew what to do. I'd dealt with plenty of bad neighbors before.

"Oh? Did you move into 422 on Thursday night?" I let him carry the bag. It was full of cans, so if he insisted, I wasn't going to argue. May as well get some use out of him.

"Yeah. Name's Herb."

I stopped at my apartment and unlocked the door. "You married, Herb?"

I'd seen the woman leaving from next door earlier. She'd worn sunglasses in the hallway, but they didn't entirely cover the purple bruise around her eye.

"Nah."

I unlocked the deadbolt. "Well, why don't you set that bag on the table?"

I put my groceries on the counter, while he closed the door and slid the chain lock closed. "You live here alone?"

You're as subtle as a sledgehammer, Herb.

"Just me and my cats. They're very shy around strangers. Probably hiding under the bed."

"Cat lady, huh?"

He stepped closer to me, invading my personal space, trying to intimidate. He stank of unwashed clothing, sweat, and nail polish remover. His knuckles were skinned up and bloody. *Had he been punching the wall last night in addition to his girlfriend? That would explain the thudding.*

I swallowed my revulsion and touched his right hand. "You need some soap and water for that. Why don't you meet me in the shower?" I tilted my head and licked my lips.

He gave me a lurid grin. "You don't fit the stereotype."

"Get the water going. Be there in a minute."

I put away the perishables and took off my clothes.

When I stepped into the shower, he was so focused on my bare breasts that he didn't notice the box cutter.

Not until I dragged it across his throat. By then, it was too late. He'd bleed out in less than a minute. The others had, anyway.

His hands went to his wounded neck, and his mouth moved. He was trying to say something, call for help, I suppose, but all he managed was a sickening gurgle.

I hated that part.

As his knees gave out, I eased him down into the tub to drain and left the shower running so the blood wouldn't clot in the drain. I'd spray it down with bleach later.

I used my electric carving knife to cut his body into seven pieces, then added his head to the collection in my freezer, shoving a package of green beans out of the way. I put each of the remaining six pieces in its own double-bagged garbage sack.

A hot shower washed all the blood off me and out of the bathtub. I got dressed in shapeless clothes, donned plastic gloves, and got to work. It was warm, and the knitted hat made my head sweat. Took three trips to get all the bags to my car—Herb was a big guy, and I had to go the long way around to avoid the doorbell camera three doors down. Spent two hours driving all over town, leaving bags in different dumpsters, miles apart from each other in down-market areas where upstanding citizens and cameras were less likely.

I took the gloves off, put them in a paper bag, and dropped them in another dumpster a block from the central police station.

I hustled back to my apartment, put on a fresh set of gloves, and got Herb's truck. I left it in long-term parking at the airport and kicked his keys down a storm drain. I paid cash for the multiple bus rides back home.

It was just getting light when I arrived. Had enough time for a few hours' sleep before I had to start cooking for the party. Peace restored, I stretched and nestled into my pillow. *Wonder if the cops will come by?* They only knocked on my door to chat that time the tuba player disappeared, and they didn't suspect a thing.

I guess I just don't fit the stereotype.

One Star - Don't Recommend

By Artemis Greenleaf

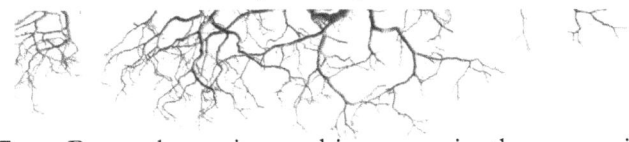

F AYE Bower knew it was him, even in the screaming ghost
mask. *Who let him on the boat for this event?*

The costumed fan handed her the book he'd just purchased.
"Can you write 'for the love of my life' in it, please?" In trying to
disguise his voice, Bryce Peterson sounded pathetic.

Faye pulled her long black hair over her shoulder before she opened the front cover and made an inscription, then
handed it back.

"Hey!" His voice was both muffled and indignant behind the
mask. "You wrote the wrong thing. Who would want 'You're in
violation of the restraining order' on their book?"

"Bryce, I know it's you. Stay away from me."

His shoulders drooped. "I will *never* give up on you. We were
meant to be together. Why can't you admit it?"

She leaned over to her bespectacled assistant, Kaden.
"Get security."

The thin young man nodded and got up.

Bryce crossed his arms. "What are they going to do? Throw
me overboard?"

"We can hope," said the lady in line behind him, dressed as
Glinda the Good Witch of the North. "Stop bothering Faye. Just
get out, creeper." She waved her star-tipped wand toward the exit.

A young woman in an event official polo and khakis jogged
up from the back of the long line. She tried using her clipboard as

a shield between Faye and Bryce, attempting to deflect him away from the author.

He dodged around her and lunged at the table. He was plucked off his feet by the iron fist of a security guard with no neck, who scruffed Bryce like a mother cat with a wayward kitten. His mask fell off, revealing unkempt dishwater blond hair and wild eyes.

"Come on, mister. Police'll be waiting for you at the dock when we return."

"Faye! Tell him! Tell him you love me, and you need me by your side!" Bryce whined as the two security men frog-marched him away.

Faye sighed and rubbed her forehead. She forced a smile at Glinda. "Sorry you had to see that."

The Good Witch handed over her copy of Faye's latest release. "I'm sorry you have to put up with that guy. What a nightmare. Loved your talk, by the way. Your books almost make me believe in the supernatural! A Halloween haunted dinner cruise for your book release party. You're brilliant!"

Faye finished signing and gave the book back. "All my publicist's idea. What was your favorite part of the meal?"

"Definitely the witch finger breadsticks. Couldn't bring myself to eat the meatball spiders."

"Yeah, those were a little too realistic. Enjoy the book and the tour of the island."

Glinda grinned as she clutched her prize to her body and headed toward the punch table. The next person in line, a medieval noblewoman, stepped up with her copy.

For the next hour and forty-five minutes, Faye signed title pages. The muscles in her hand cramped and her fingers were beginning to tingle unpleasantly when the last person in line stopped in front of her.

An announcement came over the PA system. "We are approaching Kudlow Island and will be docking soon. It was first developed as the Kudlow Lunatic Asylum in 1878 but became a tuberculosis ward in 1907. The high humidity here seemed to have an adverse effect on the patients, as they tended to expire sooner and more frequently than wards in drier climates. Kudlow was abandoned in 1921, after gaining a reputation for disappearing patients, and no one wanted to send their family members here. What actually happened was that individuals would pass during the night and their corpses would be whisked away under cover of darkness. Dr. Kudlow thought this would be less upsetting to his charges than seeing dead bodies wheeled by, but it had the opposite effect. Particularly because staff were instructed to answer all inquiries by saying the patient had begun to feel much better and had been sent home to their family. There were too many miraculous recoveries to be believed, and rumors started that the doctor was performing unethical experiments on the missing patients in a secret dungeon."

The partygoers drifted away from the dessert and coffee tables and filtered onto the deck, eager to disembark. Faye got to her feet and stretched, following the guests by way of the dessert table for a ghost pop—two strawberries on a stick, dipped in white candy bark, with black licorice eyes.

Kaden helped himself to a graveyard cupcake, picking the gummy worms off first. "What are we going to do about Bryce?"

Faye swallowed a strawberry. "I'm not sure, but we have to do something. It's bad enough he creates account after account to review-bomb my books with one star—were you able to get that last round taken down?"

"Sent all the documents. They're still working on it."

"You'd think they'd be able to auto-reject them. All copy-paste 'One Star—Don't Recommend. The author is a heartless bitch who deserves nothing.' You'd think that alone would violate terms of service."

Faye tossed the lollypop stick into the trash and headed for the deck. Kaden, still chewing the candy gravestone, was only steps behind her. He paused for a squirt of hand sanitizer at the door, then straightened his bow tie before he joined his employer in the soggy outdoors.

Chilly mist shrouded the rocky island. The dock was lit with dull, sallow lights, their pale beams directed downward onto the dark waters. Ripples from the boat shattered the reflections and scattered the shards over the top of the lake. A tall, thin woman in a white Victorian dress and ghostly pallor stood at the end of the pier. Another woman, dressed as a zombie nurse, stood slightly behind her.

The crowd flowed down the gangway onto the wooden dock. The tour guide—the woman in white—welcomed the group. Much to her consternation, Faye noted that Bryce and the two security guards stood at the rear of the group. Faye and Kaden slipped out of their places and moved quietly to the back.

"Why is he here?" Faye asked the man who'd apprehended Bryce, voice low.

"Sorry ma'am. This isn't the Merchant Marine. We don't have a brig to throw him in. Sometimes people come onto the island without permission, and security has to accompany the tour for safety." He shrugged. "Usually, it's just amateur ghost hunters, but you never know. Lot of weirdos out there. Once, we caught some devil worshipers or something like that. We were able to save the black cat they brought, but it was too late for the chicken. At least, that's what we think it was."

Faye recoiled. "I see. Thank you."

Kaden and Fay eased their way back toward the front of the group and caught the last of the safety lecture.

"... remember the tour is approximately a mile and a half walk on mostly level ground. There will be two flights of stairs. If you have any mobility issues and need assistance, please see Susan." The tour guide gestured to the scary nurse.

Susan smiled and waved, but her zombie grin was more grotesque than genial. "Thank you, Liza."

Susan opened a black trunk on the dock and removed a cardboard box. As she began to pass out battery-operated flickering candles, Liza continued with more of the island's history.

"Dr. Kudlow emigrated from the German Confederation in 1875, from the area that is now Poland. He attended the University of Gottingen with Dr. Robert Koch, who went on to isolate the tuberculosis bacterium. They corresponded frequently and Dr. Koch kept him up to date on the latest treatments and protocols. Dr. Kudlow had his own ideas when he decided to convert his lunatic asylum to a tuberculosis ward."

Susan placed the cardboard box back in the trunk and removed two battery-operated tiki torches with the same faux flames as the candles. She handed one to the tour guide.

"Now that you all have your candles, please follow me."

Liza lifted her torch and led the way toward a hulking building that loomed in the fog. The island was only about a mile long and less than half that wide. The abandoned institution was perhaps one hundred yards from the dock, but the moisture in the air was a gauzy veil obscuring the building's details.

The guide stopped at the beginning of the flagstone walkway that led to the entrance. Gas path lights along the walkway flared to life, starting with the ones closest to the tour and ending at the massive front door. An over-sized coach light depended from the vaulted ceiling of the concrete portico that framed the entrance. The red-tinted light that spilled out of it pulsated and throbbed, throwing eerie shadows across carved concrete pillars.

The man in a barbarian costume in front of Faye turned to his companion. "That looks like Hell's front porch."

Not even close.

The guide raised her torch. "I don't know how many of you watch ghost hunting shows, but Kudlow Island has been on four that we know of. There may be some unofficial ones scattered around the internet. Due to all the tragic and untimely deaths that have taken place here, it's not surprising that many people believe the building is teeming with ghosts. No one on any official tour has ever been harmed in any way by spirits. But keep in mind that we do get uninvited human guests, especially at Halloween. Please let Marcus, Donovan, or Jaimie from our security team know if you notice any suspicious activity. They're the gentlemen in red shirts." She extended her hand, and the eyes of the tour group followed its trajectory.

Three men at the back of the group raised their arms and waved.

The heavy wooden door creaked open, apparently on its own accord.

Liza lowered her torch and turned toward the building. "Let us proceed."

The foyer was open from the floor all the way to the third-floor ceiling, and the many candles of the tour group made little impact on the ocean of darkness. The room had the smell of an old structure that had been closed up for too long—not entirely unpleasant, but carrying notes of mildew, earth, and rodents.

Faye had no fear of the dead, and she and Kaden had to squeeze past the skittish crowd that hung back at the door, hesitant to step deeper into the maw of the building. Eventually, the last of the group cleared the threshold, and the door clicked shut behind them.

"We're going to continue through the lobby out to the court-yard and gardens, then tour the mortuary and return to the main building through the tunnels. The paving is a beautiful mosaic that needs to be seen from above to be truly appreciated. People claim to have seen the sobbing ghost of a nurse wandering the courtyard. Her husband was away fighting World War 1 when she fell pregnant. The father of her baby was a married doctor. Some versions of the story say she leapt to her death from the third-floor window. Others say she was pushed."

The spectral nurse had seemingly dried her tears for the evening.

As the group approached the glass French doors, they silently swung open, and Liza led them to the courtyard. It wasn't easy to tell what the mosaic was meant to represent while standing on it in a crowd of people. Even with, or perhaps in spite of, the subdued lighting, the design was something geometric, but that was all Faye could tell. Its porcelain tiles were still vibrant after all these decades. She assumed that they'd look down on it before the end of the tour.

Liza took the group through the gardens, which had provided fresh vegetables for the patients and were allegedly haunted by three young children. They must have been down for a nap.

The mortuary was surprisingly dull— thickly coated in dust, a collection of old gurneys and a broken wheelchair littered the underground room.

The tunnel back to the main building was the creepiest thing Faye had experienced in a very long time. Water dripped through the mortar between the red bricks of the walls and ceiling, leaving oily puddles on the concrete. Faye shivered in the chilly, dank air and pulled her sweater close as footsteps and voices echoed repeatedly, making the group sound three times its size. The flickering shadows cast by the candles made it appear that an army of small, misshapen creatures were crawling up the rough walls.

From time to time, Faye glanced over her shoulder. *Were Bryce and the security guards far enough away?* Even with the candles, though, it was too dark to clearly see more than one or two people behind them. The floor of the tunnel gradually sloped upward, and when Liza unlocked the wooden door, they were back in the main building,

The kitchen on the first floor was almost cheerfully bright, and supposedly haunted by a cook who'd fallen into a cauldron of boiling soup. She must have been done with tonight's meal prep.

The group took one of the grand, sweeping staircases to the second floor. Rumor had it that a nurse who'd been murdered by a combative patient from the lunatic asylum days could sometimes be heard screaming in room 254. Today was apparently her day off.

A man who'd died of TB was said to lie in a phantom bed in room 212, groaning and coughing. Obviously, he was feeling much better today.

The stairs to the third floor had an intricately carved handrail, and Faye took her time ascending so she could get a closer look at the unusual designs.

Once the entire group was assembled on the top floor, Liza began her spiel. "The first year the asylum was open, one of the patients was accidentally drowned in a therapeutic ice-water bath. He was nonverbal and well over six feet tall. Visitors have reported a tall shadow man, accompanied by wet footprints, on this floor."

She led them down the corridor to a picture window. "Please take a moment to admire the courtyard mosaic."

The tour group surged forward. Faye and Kaden hung back. Oohs and aaahs drifted toward them from the window. Dim light from the courtyard fell against the peeling, faded floral print wallpaper, and she wondered if it would have looked like a field of flowers when it was fresh and new, or just a garish jumble of blossoms.

The crowd inched forward as people took their time gazing at the paving. Liza steered the early peepers through an open door, and the hallway gradually emptied. Faye thought she and Kaden were the last two viewers.

As she moved to the window, a tall black shadow raced toward her along the wall. Startled, she let her glamour slip and hissed through needle-sharp teeth. Kaden, the spriggan, brushed one of her long, pointed ears with his wooden claws as he threw himself between her and the threat.

The shadow froze.

Faye's eyes glowed green, and Bryce cowered against the wall.

"I think I see a solution to your stalker problem." Kaden's whisper was deep and raspy.

The banshee smiled, her red lips stark against her grey teeth. "Perfect."

Kaden leaped forward and grabbed Bryce. Caught off guard, he didn't have time to so much as whimper as Kaden hurled him through the plate glass.

Faye screamed. It was a deep, keening wail of sorrow and grief that she definitely didn't feel, but it was the only voice she had.

She and Kaden stepped to the broken window. Bryce lay in the center of the courtyard, his head at an unnatural angle, and his blood trickling into the grout of the large, single star, inlaid into the courtyard.

Footsteps pounded down the hall.

Kaden slipped back into his nerdish glamour and shook his head. "One star—don't recommend."

THE GUEST

By Coda Sterling

D o you think we'll get any trick-or-treaters tomorrow?" Melody Larson tapped her fingernail idly on the doorframe.

"Doubt it." Shug knelt and ran his fingers through the ancient shag carpet. "This house has been empty for a while." He shrugged and straightened up, wiping his hands on his faded jeans. "Just leave the porch light off. That'll take care of it."

"Ha. Ha. I'll pick up a bag of candy, just in case." Her eyes dropped to the bedraggled flooring. "That carpet has to go." Melody frowned at the stained beige rug.

Her husband sighed. "We knew it was a fixer-upper. What did you expect for the bargain basement price we paid? Just hope your bed-and-breakfast idea takes off."

"Clark is coming tomorrow to help, right?"

"Yeah. He'll be here next week, when you're off, too. I'll add the rug to the to-do list. We may have to give my brother a room by the time it's all said and done."

"Maybe that'd help him get out from under your mother's thumb so he can get a girlfriend." Melody arched an eyebrow and strode into the next room.

The coffee pot gurgled the last of the hot water over the grounds. Melody poured some into her travel mug, even though it wasn't quite finished brewing. She added enough milk to make it drinkable and gave Shug a peck on the cheek.

"Let me know if you need me to pick up anything on my way home from work. Love you."

"Back at cha."

Clark was pouring his own cup of coffee and grunted his goodbye as Melody headed off to the rat race.

Melody was in a meeting with the other department heads when her phone vibrated. She discreetly looked at the message. One of her team's production servers had crashed and the failover had the data but wasn't connecting to the application database. She'd been fielding calls from angry clients all morning, and desperately hoped this was an update saying that the issue had been resolved.

It was a photo from Shug. *What is that? Not a pentagram, no star.* A thick red circle that took up most of the room had been painted on a wooden floor. Symbols she didn't recognize and words that might have been Latin filled two concentric rings around the circle. There was something else painted on the far side, but Melody couldn't tell what it was. The caption read, "Under the carpet."

Great. How many horror movies start that way? She'd reply later.

By lunchtime, the server was back up and her team had resumed their normal work projects. The afternoon slid by with no further crises, and Melody left on time. She wanted to make sure she was home with candy. Just in case. Trick-or-treat had been one of her favorite activities as a child. She and her mother had spent weeks working on her costumes, and the candy just was the frosting on the spooky cupcake.

Melody longed to make Halloween costumes with her own child. Or children. When Shug had gotten laid off from his high-powered job, the severance was enough that he didn't have to work for a while. Perhaps never, if their investment in converting this beautiful old Victorian house into a bed-and-breakfast panned out. Which would be perfect. Shug could be a stay-at-home dad. But they'd better get a move on. Her biological clock was winding down.

There was a Randall's grocery store on the way home from Melody's downtown office, so she stopped there and scoured the Halloween candy aisle. Even for a Friday, the place was deserted. It was slim pickings this late in the day, and all the premium candy was gone. She settled for a mega-bag of second-tier sweets, then picked up a few forgotten items for dinner. Melody considered the miniscule pile of discounted pumpkins and gourds but decided against buying one. It was too late to carve jack-o'-lanterns this year.

At the cash register, she grinned. Full-sized candy bars. *Yes. I want to be* that *house.* She grabbed an assorted dozen and added them to her order.

"Shug? Clark?" Melody set the groceries on the kitchen counter and grabbed a large plastic bowl to pour the candy into. She'd already turned on the front porch light.

"Up here!" her husband's voice called from the stairway.

Bowl of treats still in hand, Melody stopped in the master bedroom. She ditched her heels in the closet and retrieved her Halloween witch hat from a box on the top shelf. Just in case. *Folks are probably curious about the new owners and want an excuse to stop by, right?* She popped the hat on her head and went in search of the men.

She found them lounging in the billiards room, sipping cold craft beer.

"Hey, babe. You gotta see this." Shug got to his feet and swept her through the doorway before she could even offer them candy. Clark trailed gingerly after them.

Shug made a beeline to the back bedroom, the one that, until this morning, had sported a stained, moth-eaten beige carpet.

"Oh, wow." The occult symbols on the floor were more sinister in real life than in the photo Shug had sent. The paint was the deep blackish red of dried blood. She realized now that the symbols and words on the outside of the circle were not in concentric rings but a spiral that began with a scaly tail and ended with the head of a snake. A black diamond was painted at the center of the circle, and each apex spawned a six-pointed star with more mysterious letters inside.

Melody stepped into the room and promptly tripped over the uneven threshold and faceplanted into the circle. Her head smacked the hardwood as candy scattered across the dusty floor.

Shug winced as he leaned over to help her up. "Sorry, babe. You okay?"

"Ow ow ow!" She curled one leg in front of her and pulled a bent carpet tack from her toe, then sat and rubbed the spot on her forehead that was quickly swelling into a goose egg.

"I'll probably live. At least I got a tetanus shot after our first DIY disaster. Help me pick all this candy up so I can get an ice pack, huh?"

As the couple gathered the wayward sweets, Melody studied the other painting. Not nearly as elaborate as the one she stood in. A much smaller circle in the center of an equilateral triangle, each leg a tangent. More strange words. *I'm sure the internet knows what this is.*

Clark hung back in the hallway. "Dude, I gotta bounce. See you tomorrow."

"Later."

"Bye Melody."

His footsteps hurried across the hardwood floor, down the stairs and out the door, which he slammed behind him.

"Alrighty, then." Melody sighed, looking around the misty room. *Hadn't realized I'd kicked up so much dust.*

"What's wrong, babe?"

"I wish…" She frowned at the smear of blood near her toe. "Halloween always seems to make it worse. I just wish we would get our family started. Before it's too late. Shug, I want a baby."

The overhead light began to flicker. *Please be just a bulb. It was hard enough to get the electrician out the first time.*

Shug moved in front of her and caressed her cheek, then leaned his forehead against hers. "Yeah?"

What changed his mind from 'not yet?' "Yeah."

He bent his head and kissed her.

Something big growled from the other side of the room.

Melody's eyes snapped open, and she and Shug spun to face the sound. The light bulb flared, then exploded, showering them in glass shards and plunging the room into Stygian darkness. The paint on the floor glowed and undulated from bright red to incandescent white, as if it were a living flame.

"What the…" Words died in Shug's throat as something massive began to take shape in the darkness, starting with two glowing red eyes.

Melody watched in horror as curved horns formed above the fiery eyes, followed by a head and alarmingly broad shoulders.

"Can't you people solve your own damned problems for once?" the thing bellowed. "You are always summon—" It cocked its head and looked from Melody to Shug. "Who the hell are you?"

"We… we own the house," Shug stammered.

Did I hit my head that *hard when I fell? No way this is actually happening. Must be a dream. So, why not have fun with it?* Melody chuckled. "So, what should we call you? Lucifer? Asmodeus?"

In the pulsating light of the painted circles, she saw Shug turn toward her, but she couldn't read his expression.

"What are you doing?" he hissed in her ear.

"He can't hurt anything—he's not real. Just go with it."

The monster arched an eyebrow. "You really don't know who I am?" he crossed his beefy arms.

Melody and Shug shook their heads.

Half a smile crept over his warty face and his arms fell to his sides. "My name is… Russell." He punctuated the declaration with a sharp nod.

His name is most certainly not *Russell.* "What brings you here… Russell?"

"You did."

"How?" yelped Shug.

"The usual summoning—three drops of blood inside the circle." His eyes widened. "What is this offering?" He picked up a candy bar from the floor inside the smaller circle where he stood and passed it under his bulbous nose, sniffing it.

"It's a—" Shug started.

Russell popped the entire bar into his mouth and began chewing. He inhaled deeply and his eyes rolled upward. A goofy grin spread across his wide mouth. "Skin's a little tough, but that was sublime."

"You're supposed to take the wrapper off first." Melody tapped her top lip.

"Fine, fine. Granted."

Shug's brow furrowed. "What's granted?"

Russell threw up his hands and rolled his eyes. He sighed deeply before responding. "Your wish. What else could I possibly mean?"

"Wait, wait, wait." Melody blinked rapidly. "You grant wishes?"

"What did I just say?"

Thought that was genies, but dreams are weird. What's he going to come up with next? A juggling act? Unicorns?

Shug scratched his head. "What's the catch? What is the price of the wish?"

Russell rubbed his forehead and closed his eyes. After several moments, he exhaled loudly. "Look. I'm a wish-granting demon. It's my superpower. Which means people are *always* summoning me. Twenty-four hours a day, seven days a week. I am quite literally working like a demon." He scrunched up his face and continued in a high-pitched voice. "I want a Mercedes. Make me famous. Give me money." His face shifted back to normal. "It gets exhausting."

"But… the catch? Do you trade wishes for souls?" Shug cast a worried look at Melody.

"Souls? Really? What would I do with those?"

Melody and Shug stared at him.

"Fine. Fine. You summon me with three drops of blood and give me an offering. I grant your wish. That's it."

"You said you were a demon. There has to be more to it." Melody set the bowl of candy on the floor. Russell's glowing eyes followed it, and he licked his lips.

"You get what you wanted. Does it matter?"

"Yes," Shug and Melody said, almost in unison.

The glowing orbs of Russell's eyes narrowed. "It doesn't hurt to be as specific as possible. Cuts down on unintended consequences." Russell ran a huge, clawed hand down his face and yawned. "Is there anything else?"

"I've got to go downstairs for an ice pack. I could… make you some coffee." *I guess there's a coffee maker in my dream kitchen.*

"You would do that for me?" Russell tilted his head. "Why?"

Melody shrugged. "You're tired?"

The demon sighed. "Yes. Yes, I am. I've granted countless luxurious vacations, but never had one myself."

In the dark, Melody squeezed Shug's hand. "Well. We're converting this house to a bed-and-breakfast. Maybe… maybe you could be our first guest."

"Melody! What has gotten into you?" Shug snapped. "You can't just invite a demon into our home. I can't believe I have to tell you that."

She rubbed the lump just above her left eye. "Don't be so superstitious. Demons don't exist, Shug. Not in the real world. Ergo, this must be a dream. He's a symbol from my subconscious. But the question is: trickster or Shadow?"

Shug rubbed his forehead and sighed. "Your sister warned me about getting you that Carl Jung book last Christmas. Even if he's just the idea of a demon—"

"I accept." Hooves clicked on wood as Russell stepped out of the triangle.

"What? No!" Shug stepped in front of Melody.

"I was invited. I accepted. I'm really looking forward to my vacation. Never had one."

"Get back in your triangle!"

"No. It was Melody's blood that summoned me. Only she can command me."

"Tell him! Make him go away. Come on, babe."

"Shug… He's here for a reason. I think I need to talk with him and discover why."

"This is such a bad idea." Shug groaned. "At least… At least make him agree to abide by the house rules."

"I agree! What are the rules?"

"Well." Shug counted on his fingers, starting with the pinky. "One. No oppression. Two. No poltergeist stuff. Three. No possession." Shug hesitated, as if scrambling for the next item. "Four. No soul stealing. Five. No lurking or looming in the dark to frighten people."

"Done. I'm on vacation, remember? Why would I bring work along with me?"

Melody elbowed her husband. "Is that all?"

"For now."

"I'll put the coffee on." She started to turn toward the door, but Shug grabbed her arm. "Broken glass."

Russell snapped his fingers. There was a crystalline rattling and the fiery light reflected off fragments of glass as they soared into the air. They clicked together, and the lightbulb re-formed, bathing the room in a warm glow.

Melody rubbed her eyes. When she opened them, she couldn't stop herself from gaping at a naked Russell.

Shug grabbed her shoulders and turned her around. "Why don't you get that coffee going and put some ice on your head?" He turned to Russell. "Let me get you some clothes."

Melody eased down the stairs and held a bag of frozen peas to her head as she put a pot of coffee on. She sat at the table, propping her chin up with one forearm. The peas were starting to give her an additional type of headache.

The doorbell rang. Melody gasped. The candy was upstairs. She shambled to the front door as fast as she could go. "Just a minute!" She turned toward the stairs, only to see Shug coming down with the half-filled bowl.

Russell trailed a few steps behind him. The demon looked relaxed in Shug's white terry bathrobe. It was too small for Russell's wide frame and didn't close in the front. The sleeves stopped mid-forearm. Shug's red satin Valentine's boxers shimmered with every step.

Melody opened the door and Shug held out the bowl.

"Trick or—"

A young girl in a pink princess dress shrieked, dropped her candy tote bag, and fled to a small group of adults standing at the front gate. Two older boys, a pirate and Spiderman, peered in the half-open front door.

"Whoa!"

"That is sick!"

Melody followed their gaze to Russell.

"Where did you get that demon statue?" the pirate asked.

"Um…" Melody didn't know what to say.

Shug grinned. "Came with the house." He picked up the girl's loot bag and dropped a handful of candy inside before handing it to Spiderman.

He doled out a generous portion of sweets for each of the boys. "Happy Halloween."

As soon as they were out the front gate, he turned off the porch light.

Now that she could see Russell in the light, Melody wondered where her brain had come up with that fever dream. Dark red skin matched the color of the floor markings upstairs. His torso was a parody of a man's—over-broad at the shoulder and too narrow at the hip. Heavily muscled. His legs, covered in dark curly hair, bent backward at the knees and ended in cloven hooves. He had two sets of muscular arms: an expected pair at his shoulders and a smaller pair stuck out of the robe just above his waist. The hands at the ends of the arms were wide and clawed. Tips of leathery wings peeked over his shoulders.

Russell's face was both terrifying and comical. His pronounced chin seemed to Melody a caricature of a strong chin. Between it and the prominent brow ridge, his head reminded her of a crescent moon. Lumpy and bumpy, his skin was like one of those warty pumpkins the grocery store had marked down to half price when Melody was there earlier. Ice pick-sharp black horns curved toward each other from the sides of his head, nearly meeting in the middle.

Shug guided Melody to the recliner, where she sat and held the now half-thawed bag of frozen peas to her head. It was the last thing she remembered until the alarm began to chirp.

Melody groped for the beeping phone on her nightstand. "Ow!" Her hand flew to the lump on her forehead, where she probed gingerly. "I guess at least that part really happened."

After silencing the alarm, she rolled over to tell Shug about her weird dream. He was already up. *Huh. He normally sleeps in on a Saturday.*

She dressed and headed downstairs with a basket of laundry. The divine aroma of French vanilla coffee wafted up the stairs to greet her. She had to go through the kitchen to the utility room, anyway, so she might solve the mystery of Shug's early awakening.

Melody screamed and dropped the basket. "What the…?"

Russell and Shug turned to her. Russell looked up from his plate of scrambled eggs and grinned.

Shug, loading the dishwasher, looked at his wife and shook his head. "I told you."

"Demons… Demons. Aren't. Real. This is not happening."

"I'm as real as they come, hon." Russell speared two pieces of bacon before he picked up the tablet lying next to his plate and started reading as he chewed.

"You invited him to be our houseguest, remember?"

"That was just a dream!"

"It wasn't."

It had to have been a dream. Except… how would Shug know what happened inside my dream? Melody blinked rapidly and tried to force herself to take deep breaths. Once her knees felt strong enough to support her weight, she picked up the basket and made her way across the kitchen.

When she returned from starting the washer, she stood as near to Russell as she dared. "So. Russell. You have anything in mind for today? Hiking? Arboretum?"

He looked up from the device. "Not a fan of sunlight, Mel. Besides, what do you think people would do if they saw me out and about? Nope. After breakfast, I'm going to kick back and watch some TV."

"TV?"

"Sure. Alvin here was giving me some suggestions."

Alvin. Melody tripped over the name. She heard it so rarely. When Melody and Shug first graduated from college, she earned more than he did. By a lot. Still, people assumed he was the breadwinner. She jokingly started referring to him as her sugar daddy, and the nickname stuck, albeit in shortened form, even after his night school MBA granted him the key to the executive washroom. Almost everyone called him 'Shug,' even his brother.

"Okay, then. You boys have fun. I'm gonna run some errands while the washer's going."

Melody pulled up next to the donation bin behind the grocery store. Looking at the bags in front of it she wondered if the dumpster was full, or if people were just lazy. She unloaded the first bag and went back for the second.

From somewhere behind her, a coughing and squeaking erupted.

Is that… a baby crying? She stepped over to the piles of donations. One of the bags moved. Melody gasped and untied the loose knot. A baby squirmed and wailed inside the plastic.

Shhhhhh. She scooped the child into her arms. "I'll get help. Don't worry. It's going to be okay."

Melody jogged around to the front of the store. *How could someone do this?*

The store manager called 9-1-1 and sent someone to get diapers off the shelf in Aisle 17. As the manager put the diaper on the little girl, Melody couldn't help but notice a big lump just inside the child's hip bone.

Wrapped in an acrylic Halloween print throw, the baby started to settle as Melody rocked her back and forth. "You think she's hungry?"

The manager tilted her head. "Probably best to wait until the paramedics get here to check her out."

Melody nodded and kept rocking.

The ambulance soon arrived to whisk the baby away to the hospital. A police officer took her statement.

She folded the paper the officer gave her and pushed it into her purse. "What's going to happen to her?"

"After the hospital checks her out, CPS will place her until any family's found."

"The family that threw her in the dumpster?"

He shrugged. "We don't really know what happened, do we?"

"Guess not. Is there anything else you need from me?"

"No, ma'am."

Melody struggled to hold back tears on the way to her car. She'd been aching for a baby of her own, while someone else callously threw a precious little girl in a plastic donation bag to die. *Why is life so cruel sometimes?*

As Melody drove home, the officer's words played over and over in her head. *CPS will place her...* Could she and Shug take care of her? Until her relatives were found, of course. She made an illegal U-turn and sped toward the emergency room.

The hospital social worker leaned back in her chair. "Are you sure? Nobody's exactly lining up to adopt terminally ill babies."

Melody bit her lip. "Yes, Mrs. Johnson. If you can't find her people, we—my husband and I—would be honored to take care of her. I think it's wrong for a baby to have to go through this alone. She's already had a rough start."

Shug said 'yes' to a baby. If Russell wasn't a dream, then that wasn't, either. Even if it's only for a short time, this little girl needs me.

Melody blinked away the moisture welling in her eyes. "Have you given her a name?"

"Officially, she's still 'Baby Doe,' but one of the nurses said she reminded her of a song, so I've been calling her Lyric."

Lyric belongs with Melody!

Mrs. Johnson opened a desk drawer and pulled out a packet of forms. "Here you go. Normally, it takes a couple of months to get approved, but given the circumstances, I think I can expedite the application. We'll get the ball rolling when you bring back the notarized documents."

"Can I visit her in the hospital while that's happening? Does she even have a couple of months?"

"Honestly… I don't know. Depends on how she responds to treatment. Please know that there may not be anything they can do for her, other than palliative care. Look, the hospital always needs volunteers to hold sick babies. Stop by the information desk on your way out. They'll get you registered for NICU nursery helpers and give you a list of vaccinations you'll need."

Melody completed the forms that didn't need Shug's signature and left. At the front desk, she filled out another stack of forms and signed up for the training class that started on Monday at 11 AM. *Is it dumb luck that I've already scheduled time off?*

Armed with her checklist, she adjusted her route to go home via the pharmacy for the jabs.

By the time Melody walked through the front door, her arm ached from the shots and the bump on her forehead throbbed from emotions that wobbled on the knife edge of control. She was barely holding it together, and all she wanted was to feel Shug's comforting arms around her as she told him about Lyric.

Peals of laughter greeted her. She followed the sound into the kitchen, where she found Shug, Russell, and Clark sitting around the table. The brothers had playing cards stuck to their foreheads. Russell's was cradled in his horns. Beer cans took up a large portion of the table surface, and empties were scattered on the floor.

"Hey, babe!" Shug's voice boomed, too loud.

"Hey." She turned around, ran up the stairs and took a long, hot shower, crying until no more tears came. Fearing that in the silence her thoughts would overwhelm her again, she grabbed her ear buds and listened to a podcast until she fell asleep.

A loud *snork* from Shug woke Melody. He only snored when he was drunk. Through the picture window, the velvet black of the night sky was just starting to give way to the grey dawn. She got up and headed to the bathroom, shaking her head at her puffy eyes and the shrinking lump on her forehead in the mirror as she washed her hands. *May as well get up.*

She got dressed and padded down the stairs, dreading to see what the kitchen looked like. A white crew sock lay at the foot of the staircase. Its mate was scrunched up a few feet away. Melody's nose wrinkled. *Did they cut up onions last night?*

A dark crumpled item rested on the floor about halfway to the kitchen. Melody picked it up. *Uggggh*. She dropped the black cotton boxers and shook her hand, as if trying to get rid of crawling bugs. *What happened there? Smells like sulfur and something dead. Ewww.*

She retrieved the broom and dustpan, then swept up the pungent underpants and dropped them in the garbage. Gave her hands a double wash before she got the coffee going.

The kitchen was a disaster area. Sink full of dishes. Beer cans on the table and floor. An empty bottle of whiskey on the counter. Pothos ivy knocked over.

Shug, Clark, and Russell made the mess. They could clean it up, hangovers or no. She did right the plant and pat the soil back into place, though.

It was pleasantly cool, this second day of November, and Melody took her coffee out on the patio. She sipped and wondered how Lyric was doing this morning as the sunrise bled across the horizon. The solution seemed obvious. She had a wish-granting demon under her roof. She would just wish Lyric was healthy and free of cancer. That she and Shug could adopt her.

But the warning Russell had given them gave her pause. *'It doesn't hurt to be as specific as possible. Cuts down on unintended consequences.'* It had been gnawing at the back of her mind all along, the unsettling idea that she had wished for a baby and the next day, one practically fell into her lap. Before Friday, she would have just brushed it off as an odd coincidence. Now, she wasn't so sure. A tear rolled down her cheek as she recalled the lump on Lyric's hip. *Were all the wishes Russell granted tainted? Or had Fate placed this baby with no chance in her path so she could be healed with a magic wish?*

Melody rubbed her arms. The 'pleasantly cool' had gradually changed into 'too cool.' She had grocery shopping to do. *Wouldn't hurt to get that done before the boys roll out of bed and the store gets busy.*

She tiptoed upstairs to get her purse and noticed someone lying on the floor in the summoning room. Melody trotted over to see who it was, and her hand flew to her mouth.

Her brother-in-law was sprawled in the magic circle.

"Clark!" She knelt and shook his shoulder. "Clark?"

Mmmmmmngh. He opened one eye. "What?"

Melody let out a relieved sigh. "I thought… never mind. Why don't you go get in bed in the blue room?" She looked around at the symbols on the floor. "What were you doing in here last night?"

"I don't really remember."

He struggled to his feet and then grabbed Melody's shoulder for balance. He looked her in the eye and made a face. "You look like shit."

She winced at his dragon breath. "Thanks. And you wonder why women won't talk to you."

He waved dismissively and staggered off to find a bed.

By the time Shug and Russell came down, Melody had shopped, put away the groceries, taken a nap, and vacuumed downstairs. Except the kitchen. She wasn't touching that. She was relaxing in the living room, feet on an ottoman, watching TV.

Russell headed straight for the kitchen. Shug stood in the doorway, peering at her.

Melody clicked the pause button. "Good morning!"

Shug squinted. "So. Loud." He grimaced and rubbed his temples. "Morning." He moved to sit next to her on the loveseat then reached out to touch her cheek. "Are you okay?"

"Shug, we need to talk."

He swallowed. "What's wrong? Are you upset about last night? It was just—"

"No!" Melody closed her eyes for a moment. "It's nothing to do with that." She took his hand and told him about Lyric.

Fortunately, Shug had agreed to adopt Lyric by the time Clark shambled down the stairs.

"Is there any coffee?" He interrupted the remains of their conversation.

"Let me show you how to make it." Melody got up and led the way to the kitchen.

Russell stood near the open refrigerator door, in all his naked glory, drinking milk out of the carton. He gave a satisfied burp and put it back in the fridge.

Melody's lip curled. "Was that your underwear on the floor?"

"Yep!" Russell grinned and slapped his belly with both hands. "The boys had to breathe."

"Okay, can they breathe in the privacy of your room, please? And why are you drinking out of the carton? I just bought that. And now… it's all yours."

"Well, you had to go to the store anyway. You're out of bread, eggs, and bacon."

"I just went to the store this morning! How are we out?"

Russell shrugged. "I made breakfast."

Melody wanted to shriek at Russell. *With a dozen eggs? Two pounds of bacon? An entire loaf of bread?* But she gritted her teeth. *Is this what my future holds as a B&B host?* "Okay. I hope you left yourself something for supper. It's the first Sunday of the month, and we always have dinner with Shug and Clark's parents." Russell started to open his mouth, and she felt she needed to nip his dining aspirations in the bud. "At a restaurant. I'll leave you gentlemen to tidy up after yourselves."

Melody stood next to Joni Larson, Shug's mother, in the restaurant parking lot. Joni's friend, Inez, stood on the other side. She had been Joni's best friend forever and often joined them on their first-Sunday dinners. Shug, Clark, and their father, John, gathered around the open hood of Inez's car. It would start but stall out after a few seconds.

Inez shifted her purse strap. "Do any of them actually know anything about fixing cars?"

"Not as far as I know," Joni replied.

Inez unzipped her bag. "I'm calling roadside assistance."

Her call only took five minutes, but she sighed heavily when she hung up. "At least forty-five minutes."

"Oh. Oh, that's too long. John has to take his medicine before then. But I can't just leave you here."

Melody cleared her throat. "Why don't you ask Clark to wait with Inez? He can run her home once the tow truck picks up her car."

"Excellent idea." Joni nodded to her friend.

"Do you think he'll mind?" Inez glanced over at the men.

"Not at all. Besides, since you're staying at our house, it'll be even closer for him."

"Is everything okay, Inez?" Melody hoped she hadn't developed a medical condition or anything serious since the last time they'd met.

"Fumigating my house for termites."

"Ah."

Joni walked over to the car and explained the plan. Clark looked like he was going to argue but glanced over at Inez and forced a smile instead.

Melody and Shug sat at the kitchen table with their morning coffee, peeling oranges. Half a bag of easy-peel mandarins was the only food left in the house.

"How long is Russell going to be here again, babe?"

Melody rubbed her forehead, smearing juice in her hairline. "I don't think we actually discussed that."

Something squeaked upstairs. Then again. And again. They both looked at the ceiling.

Shug quirked an eyebrow, followed by a knowing smile. "That sounds like…"

"Bedsprings?" Melody offered.

"Wonder if the tow truck driver was a lady?"

A deep groan followed. They both gaped at the ceiling.

Melody was the first to speak. "You don't think…? Clark and…?"

Shug only stared at her, eyes wide and mouth open.

Hooves clopped on the linoleum. "You know, that yoga is something else. A good stretch'll make you feel like a million bucks." Russell threw back his head and let out another groan.

"Wait." Shug glanced at the demon, then back up to the ceiling. His shoulders dropped. "If you're down here, who's up there?"

Russell chuckled. "Better answer the door."

"The door?"

An urgent pounding came from the front door. Russell started up the stairs as Shug and Melody hurried to the entryway. Joni pushed her way inside as soon as Shug turned the lock.

"Mom? What's wrong?"

"Is Clark here? I have to talk to him."

"He's not up yet. Let me go get him." Shug closed the door.

Joni was already halfway to the stairs.

"Mom, wait!"

"No time."

Melody moved closer to Shug. "This is going to be awkward."

Upstairs, a door was flung open. Then a loud gasp. Melody and Shug both cringed.

"Inez? What are you…? Why is Clark naked? Oh. My. God."

Melody clapped her hand over her mouth. Shug stood with his jaws agape, as if trying to parse what they had both just heard.

Joni stormed down the stairs, Inez, wrapped in a sheet, in hot pursuit. Clark trotted after the women, holding a lacy floral pillow in front of his twig and berries.

"Mom! Wait. Let me explain."

Joni did not stop until she reached the bottom of the stairs. She whirled to face Inez, who nearly crashed into her.

"How dare you? You have known my son since I was pregnant with him. And to think I was worried when you didn't come home last night. You… you cradle robber!"

Joni strode toward the door, pausing long enough to shake a finger at Shug. "You let this happen."

"They're both adults, Mom," Shug ventured half-heartedly.

The door slammed in his face.

Melody's phone alarm sounded. "I've got to get to class!"

Melody dropped off the notarized paperwork with Mrs. Johnson on her way to the NICU. The orientation went well and she was eager to visit Lyric. Sadly, the baby was fussy and uncomfortable.

A nurse came to check on IVs. "She's scheduled for surgery Wednesday to remove the tumor. Takes up most of her pelvis."

Melody rubbed the infant's eyebrows. "Poor Lyric. You'll feel much better after it's gone."

The nurse gave her a grim smile. "If she survives the surgery." She squeezed Melody's shoulder and left to continue her rounds.

Lyric cried and squirmed. Melody tried everything she'd learned in class. Rocking. Walking. Bouncing. The only thing that seemed to help was singing quietly to her. She kept control until her shift ended and she got to her car. Tears streamed down her cheeks the entire way home. She knew what she had to do.

Inez and Clark sat next to each other at the dinner table, holding hands and laughing. They were in their own little bubble, scarcely interacting with Melody and Shug. Clark had persuaded Russell to have a pizza feast in his room while Inez was there.

The price of his compliance was high—five large pies in assorted configurations—but Clark had happily shelled out for the delivery.

"Potatoes, please." Clark pointed his fork at the dish of au gratin.

Shug passed them but held on until his brother met his eyes. "You talked to Mom?"

"Giving her a few days to cool off."

Melody could understand why Joni was upset. It must have been very shocking for her to walk in on her best friend and her son in flagrante delicto. But Shug was also right. They were both adults. At 32, Clark was far from being a child. Joni was 58, so Melody figured Inez was a similar age.

"That must have been some tow truck ride."

Inez nodded. "The 45-minute wait turned out to be almost two hours. We sat in the restaurant bar and talked until he showed up. Then we dropped Clark's car here and walked down to Mamacita's. The two-for-one Margaritas were way stronger than they had any right to be." Clark squeezed her hand and she beamed at him. "I regret nothing."

"Me either," he added.

After the meal was finished, Inez and Melody stepped into the living room while Shug and Clark cleaned the kitchen.

They both sat on the couch. Melody wanted to talk to Russell before she lost her nerve, not play hostess. Without thinking, she reached for the remote.

"Melody?" Inez bit her lip. "I want to level with you. I don't know what's going to happen with me and Clark. We may be done tomorrow, or it could last for years. I mean, he may want a family, and I'm..." She shrugged. "I know Joni's disappointed. I get that. Really." Inez sighed and paused as if searching for the right words.

"When my husband left me for a woman the same age as our daughter, that almost did me in. I felt so old and worthless. Like litter on the side of the road. Like a ghost, haunting my own life, invisible and unheard. And then Clark happened. I haven't been this happy in a long time. I would do it again in a heartbeat."

"He's a good guy." Melody gave a gentle nod. "Clark has been very lonely for a while now. He deserves to be happy, too."

"Doesn't everybody?"

That's when the dam broke and the story of desperately wanting a baby and then finding Lyric came spilling out. Inez put her arm around Melody's shoulders as she hung on every word.

The sound of the dishwasher starting caused Melody to break off her story. "I think they're done. I'm glad we had a chance to talk, Inez. I hate to be a wet blanket, but I feel like I have a migraine coming on and I need to go lie down." Melody hated the lie, but she couldn't exactly tell Inez what she was really going to do.

"Hope you feel better soon."

"Thanks."

Melody hurried up the stairs before Shug and Clark came out of the kitchen. Taking a deep breath and letting it out slowly, she knocked on Russell's door.

"What is it, Mel?"

"Can I come in?"

"Door's open."

She slipped inside his room, then gawked at the array of empty pizza boxes.

The demon lounged on the bed in the altogether, picking his teeth with a claw. "What can I do you for?"

"Russell, I know you're on vacation, and I wouldn't ask unless it was really important."

"It's about Lyric, isn't it?"

Melody didn't recall telling him about the baby, but she supposed he could have overheard her talking to Shug. "She needs a miracle. She's scheduled for surgery on Wednesday, and even if she survives it, her prognosis isn't good. I want a wish. I want you to heal her. Put her to perfect health. Make it so Shug and I can adopt her. With no unintended consequences, side effects, loopholes, etcetera. She's whole and healthy, we adopt her, and she's part of our big happy family. Nothing else."

"Not sure I can do that, Mel. Altering someone's fate isn't the same as conjuring a new Rolls Royce."

Melody's eyes flashed. "What if it was Fate that brought both of you into my life at the same time? I never believed in demons until you showed up, so Fate could also be a thing."

Russell shrugged. "Correlation does not prove causation."

"What about Clark? He wished for a girlfriend, didn't he?"

"That's different. They were both looking for love. I just put them in each other's way. They did the rest."

"Please, Russell. It's a matter of life or death."

"Is that all?"

"It's enough, isn't it?"

The demon stared at Melody with fire-bright eyes. "What are you offering for this wish?"

"Well, I've already offered you a room in my house for your vacation. What more do you want? Money? Sex? My soul?"

"There you go with the souls again." He shook his head. "I don't *need* money, and frankly, you aren't my type."

"Fine. What *do* you want?" Frustration edged Melody's voice.

Russell crossed his arms and pursed his lips. "I usually ask that question. Feels weird to be answering it." He drummed his claws on his muscular arm. "Chocolate. There is no chocolate where I come from."

"I wouldn't think so," Melody muttered. "Okay. I'll get you some chocolate. Do you have a preference?"

"I don't understand."

"Dark chocolate? Milk chocolate? Chocolate with nuts? Bonbons, cremes, liqueur?"

"Yes."

"Okay. Deal." Melody closed the door behind her and hurried to the store.

She returned with a shopping bag filled with almost every variety of chocolate the grocery had.

Russell's eyes widened as she came into his room, then his shoulders drooped. "I'm not sure I can fulfill this bargain."

"Why not?"

"You are making a wish for someone else, not yourself. I cannot interfere with a person's free will."

"Lyric is a tiny baby. She can't even talk, much less understand what free will is. You're going to let her die because she can't consent to be healed?"

Russell shrugged. "I don't make the rules." He cocked his head. "Do you think souls are just randomly stuffed into bodies and sent to this plane just for shits and giggles?"

Melody's forehead wrinkled. "Never really thought about it."

Russell nodded. "Really? I wouldn't have guessed. Leave the chocolate. I'll see what I can do. Come back at midnight, and I'll let you know."

She handed the bag over and left. The bedsprings in Clark's room were squeaking again, so she hurried by. It seemed voyeuristic to listen.

Downstairs, Shug was playing a game on his computer. Fearing she would burst into tears if she talked to him, she diverted into the kitchen. With two hours and a megawatt of nervous energy to kill, she began reorganizing the cupboards.

At 11:59, Melody knocked on Russell's door. It was ajar and swung open when she touched it.

"Russell?"

There was no reply, so she stepped inside and flicked the switch. Russell was gone, but candy wrappers were scattered all over the floor. He'd eaten every crumb of chocolate she'd bought. Melody frowned. *You couldn't just put your trash in the bag?*

There was something on the dresser. It appeared to be one of those big glass paperweights that is cut to look like a diamond. There was a note underneath it, written in blood red ink.

Melody/Alvin

Thanks for the vacay. It's been nice, but I'm starting to get bored. Idle hands etc. See you next time (and there's always a next time).

Russell

Melody felt her heart break and she sniffled. "I guess that's a no." Her misty eyes fell on the paperweight. *Where did this come from?* She picked it up.

The room disappeared.

She found herself in an empty space. Perhaps not entirely empty. There was a solid floor to walk on, but it was either black or clear, letting the blackness below show through. As far as she could see in any direction—nothingness.

"Hello? Russell? Is this some kind of joke?"

There was no reply, not even an echo. Melody began to walk. She paused to call out from time to time, but never got an answer. Occasionally, she thought she heard someone call her name, or footsteps, or whispering behind her, but no matter how fast she turned, she was alone. Completely alone.

Am I dead?

No answer came to her, but she saw a tiny glowing speck on the horizon, so she pushed down her fear and hurried toward it.

As she got closer, the speck became sand. Palm trees swayed in a gentle breeze around a shimmering blue pool of water, fed by a spring that flowed from a boulder. Flowers blossomed in shades of red, orange, and yellow.

Melody's bare feet touched the oasis sand. It was warm, almost unpleasantly so. She ran to the water, but found she had no reflection. She looked down to confirm that her body was still there.

"Hello, Melody." A woman had come out from behind the rock and approached.

Melody took a step backward. "Who are you? What is this place?"

The newcomer stopped about three feet away. Clad in a gauzy sheath dress, she had olive skin and an hourglass figure. Her hair was made of vines that writhed on their own. Flowers erupted, then turned to fruit, which ripened, withered, and dropped away, only to start the cycle again.

"You could say I am Russell's supervisor."

Melody swallowed hard. "Am I in Hell?"

"That depends. Do you want to be?"

"What? No! Of course not."

"Chaos."

"This place?"

The woman laughed. "*I* am Chaos."

Melody couldn't help but stare at Chaos' eyes. They shifted color every time she blinked, and Melody was fascinated by the ever-changing display.

"Russell had to escalate your service request to management."

Lyric! "And?" Melody felt strangely calm.

"I can't just grant an override, but your business is important to us. I'll try to facilitate your request, but please understand that all agreements are final and there are no refunds."

Chaos lunged forward and pushed Melody into the pool. She tried to swim toward the surface, but something pulled her down into the fathomless depths. Her lungs screamed for air, and she fought against her body's reflex to breathe as she thrashed her arms and kicked. But she continued down into the darkness. Her jaw forced its way open and icy water flowed into Melody's mouth.

With a gasp, she sat up in her own bed. Shug stirred and turned over.

Melody's hands shook so hard that she almost dropped her keys on the way to the car. Today might be the last time she ever saw Lyric. She would wait during the surgery tomorrow, hoping the baby made it through, but today, the only thing she could do was hold her. And sing a lullaby or two.

She signed in and hurried to the NICU. Lyric's bassinet was empty.

Melody swallowed the lump in her throat and fought back tears.

The nurse from yesterday was making an entry on the tablet she carried with her a few beds over.

"Excuse me? Ma'am? Could you tell me what happened to the little girl that was over there—Baby Doe?"

"Oh, she's in the regular ward now. Strangest thing. This morning, her tumor was just gone. Did an ultrasound, couldn't find a trace of it. They re-did her bloodwork, and it was all normal."

Before Melody could respond, her phone rang. "Mrs. Johnson?"

"Melody! I have good news. I was able to push through the emergency foster approval. I'm going to do a home visit tomorrow at ten AM. If you pass, you can take custody of Lyric immediately."

"Thank you."

"Just make sure you go over the checklist in the packet I gave you. See you tomorrow."

Melody stood blinking away tears.

It was a Halloween miracle!

If you enjoyed this book, please consider leaving a review at your favorite book site. Reviews help other readers find and enjoy new books!

To explore more content from Artemis Greenleaf, A.B. Richards, and Coda Sterling, please visit BlackMareBooks.com

For more works from David Welling, please visit DavidWelling.com